SECRET OF COFFIN ISLAND

MARIE BARTEK & THE SIPS TEAM BOOK 4

ROBIN MURPHY

I love crime, I love mysteries, and I love ghosts

STEPHEN KING

ONE

THE OCEAN WAVES pounded out a rhythm that soothed your soul as its spray danced in the air with the seagulls. Crystal-like sands glistened in the sun as the sea slowly melted away the shore. With each ripple of water, the sand eroded away the remains of the coffins revealing headless skeletons facing west. Tiny sand crabs scurried in and out of the chest cavities and nibbled on century-old plankton and bacteria. The smell of decay mixed with salt gave out a sulfur-like odor even too putrid for the beach animals to ignore, while the sound of a sword sliced through the air...

"Marie, are you listening? Marie, can you hear me? Where did you go just now?" Gale Winters waved her hand in front of Marie's dazed eyes.

Dr. Marie Bartek shook her head in a startled rattle and focused her eyes on Gale. "What, oh sorry, I just had the strangest vision."

"Seriously, today you have a strange vision? Marie, it's your wedding day and the ever so handsome Chief Cory Miller awaits you at the other end of the hall." Gale looked at Helen Bartek and shook her head. "Can you please talk some sense into your daughter? I give up. I'm having enough difficulty fixing her hair."

"Gale, I gave up talking sense into Marie a long time ago." Helen leaned over and patted Marie's hand. "Are you sure you're okay?"

"Mom I'm fine, sorry to have upset you. I'm still learning about these psychic abilities myself."

Helen leaned forward and lightly brushed her daughter's cheek. "You look absolutely radiant. Wait until your father sees you, he won't be able to keep it together walking you down the aisle."

Marie smiled and stared at her mother's hazel eyes and golden hair and thought she looked amazing for her age. "I'm thrilled I come from such a great gene pool. You and dad look amazing for your age."

Gale walked back over with a lip-gloss wand in her hand and grabbed Marie's chin. "Stop talking, I can't do your makeup with you zoning out into la-la land and moving your head. So, are you going to tell us where you were just now? Don't answer until I'm done here."

Marie crossed her eyes and waited until Gale finished. "My, aren't you the bossy one today? As to where I was, I have no clue. I saw the beach, and it was beautiful and serene, and then I saw a row of headless skeletons and tiny crabs crawling in and out of the chest cavities."

Gale stopped smiling and raised her eyebrows. "You saw what? Wow, now that is really creepy and not what you should be thinking about on your wedding day. Can you put that on hold for a while?"

"How does Cory deal with all of this?" Helen got up and began to fidget with her bracelet.

Marie walked over and lovingly placed a hand on her mother's shoulder as she shook her head at Gale. "I'm okay, and Cory's more than okay. Don't worry about all of this. Gale's right, I'm getting married in less than an hour, time to focus on that."

Gale replied, "Right, now I'd like to make some final touches on myself if that's okay? I'm still trying to keep Tim's attention. I have a reputation to uphold."

Marie chuckled and waited until her mother was out of earshot as she whispered to Gale. "I think I saw something about those bodies that were found here on Folly Island back in nineteen eighty-seven."

"Yeah, I was going to ask you that, but figured it wasn't a good idea for your mom to hear anymore. Do you think it means anything? I mean, it usually does."

"I don't know yet, these are the times I miss Myra, especially today."

Gale grabbed Marie's shoulders and said, "Now look, we both know Myra is here. I know you mean you wished she were here on this side, but she's here in spirit. You of all people should know that. Don't start doubting your belief system now, okay? Now come on, you're gonna mess up all the hard work I put into your makeup."

Marie nodded her head and turned to look into the cognac-stained oval floor mirror. Her highlighted blonde hair was coiled at the top of her head as ringlets cascaded at the neck. Her emerald eyes were softly hidden beneath her veil as they glistened with happiness and pride. "I'm so glad I chose this dress in ivory. It's simple and elegant and actually allows me to breathe."

Helen walked over and stood beside Marie and

3

smiled. "I wasn't sure if I would like the halter empire waist, but the beading is magnificent, and you look like a princess."

Gale spoke as she added rose blush to her cheeks. "I love the way it cinches up the back and how the satin flares out just below the hips. To me, you look like a mermaid. You're always swimming in the ocean anyway, so a perfect fit."

"You would say I look like a mermaid." Marie turned to face her mother and best friend as she picked up her bouquet filled with pink Astilbe, purple Zinnias, and a touch of white Shasta Daisies and Cosmos.

Helen reached into her purse and pulled out a square black velvet box and handed it to Marie. "The jewelry inside this box belonged to your great-grandmother. She wore it on her wedding day just as my mother and I did. I've been waiting for this day to pass it on to you to carry out the tradition. We have all had strong and loving marriages. I hope it brings the joy that you and Cory deserve."

Marie's hands shook as she opened the box and saw a simple pearl necklace and earrings. "Oh mother, this is absolutely beautiful. I don't know what to say. I never saw this around the house when I was growing up."

"That's because they've been stowed away in a safe deposit box. Marie, these are very valuable. Please take good care of them, and I hope I'm alive to see you hand them off to your daughter on her wedding day."

Marie leaned in and kissed her mother's cheek. "Thank you, and I love them."

Gale grabbed a tissue and wiped the corners of

her eyes. "Okay, now that's enough. We're all going to need a makeover. I'm never going to make it through the ceremony."

Marie wrapped her arms around her mother and best friend and took in a deep breath. She stood an inch less than Gale who claimed to be five foot nine. "Okay ladies, let's do this. Let me meet my soul mate and make this official."

They all laughed and walked out of the room toward the end of the hall to meet Marie's father. Gale's charcoal black hair draped over her bare shoulders, and her olive skin tone complimented the chiffon deep plum gown, which was an elegant contrast to Helen's classic chiffon taupe suit with beaded collars and cuffs.

Marie's father, Paul Bartek, stood tall and proud wearing a simple black tuxedo with a charcoal gray tie. He smiled wide as a tear slipped out the corner of his eye when he leaned forward to kiss Marie on the cheek. "You look just like your mother did on her wedding day. I couldn't be more proud to walk you down that aisle."

Marie choked back her tears so she wouldn't look like a raccoon when she exchanged her vows. "Oh Daddy, I'm excited and scared to death at the same time. Is that normal?"

"Absolutely, so take my arm and lean on me, just as you always did when you were little. I want you to know that I'll always be here for you to lean on, both your mother and I will."

Marie leaned her head on his shoulder and smiled. "I know and thank you. I can't imagine not having you and Mom here to share this day with me."

Marie watched her older brothers Edward and

Warren escort her mother to the front of the small chapel. She caught a glimpse of Cory and Tim Haines standing at the altar before the doors slowly closed.

Marie and Cory chose to have a simple June beach wedding, and it was only natural to have Gale and Tim as the maid of honor and best man. The white and red baby roses had been arranged on the altar in a solid brass vase trimmed with satin plum bows.

The Folly Beach United Methodist church was a quaint white wood-sided chapel that barely seated a hundred people. It was quietly tucked in amongst the palm trees and a short distance to the South Carolina oceanfront beach house where the wedding reception would take place.

An hour later, Marie and Cory walked out through the opened church doors as friends and family members blew bubbles into the air. The wedding was traditional and progressive at the same time, and all the planning and organizing was worth any amount of money and arguing with Gale over details. Now it was time to head to the reception and party with everyone who meant the world to them.

Cory stared at the string of cans tied to the back bumper of his British racing green convertible MG. "You all do realize this is a classic?"

Gale sheepishly grinned and said, "Yeah we know, heaven forbid should we leave any marks on the precious car. Look, we placed bubble wrap on the bumper before we tied the string."

Tim pumped up his chest and saluted Cory. His six-foot-five frame stretched the seams of his tuxedo. "That was my idea. This was the least damage I would allow her to do. She wanted to blow up condoms and tie them to the mirrors."

"Allow me to do?" Gale grabbed Tim's tie and yanked him against her body. "Nobody *allows* me to do anything. Got that?"

Marie shook her head. "Oh, trust me, we've all got that."

"Okay everyone, I think we have enough pictures here at the church. It's time to head over to the reception." Helen tapped Marie's arm and winked. "I'm glad there are no condoms tied to anything."

"Yeah, I am too. Okay, let's go, I'm starving. Plus, I need a glass of wine." Marie lifted the folds of her dress and draped them over her arm and ever so carefully slid down into the moss-leathered upholstery.

Their car horns blew at passersby as they sped off toward the beach and Marie laughed at the cans bouncing and clanking against the road. She felt the warm sun against her face as the breeze lightly dried her glossed lips. Her heart felt as if it would explode with love and pride now that she was officially Mrs. Cory Miller. Or was it Mrs. Chief Cory Miller? Those were details to iron out when she wrote out their thank you cards.

"I can smell the ocean." Cory grabbed Marie's hand and pulled her knuckles to his lips. "Well, Mrs. Miller, are you ready for the rest of our lives?"

"Oh, I'm more than ready." Marie gazed at his deep brown eyes and sandy brown hair and leaned her head on his shoulder. "It was so kind of your cousin to allow us to use their beach house for our reception. I can't imagine a more fitting place to celebrate."

"I would skip everything to have you all to myself.

Why don't we pretend to have headaches and disappear?"

"Yeah, we need a code word, so we know when we're on the same page. How about potato salad?"

"Potato salad, where on earth did you come up with that, and are we even having potato salad at the reception?"

Marie belly laughed and said, "I have no idea, but if you hear me say it, it's time to retreat. Oh, and I'd like to thank you again for agreeing to move into my house. I know it was tough for you to give up your condo."

"It wasn't that difficult, I mean come on, a tiny condominium facing an alley as opposed to living on the beach? It was an obvious choice." Cory downshifted to second gear. "I didn't want to upset you, but have you seen Myra at all?"

Marie lifted her head and heavily sighed. "No, I haven't. She was coming through for me so clearly up until about a month before the wedding. I don't understand it. Plus, I could really use her help because I had the oddest vision right at the church before the wedding."

"About what?"

"About headless skeletons in coffins buried in the sand."

"You're kidding, right? That sounds like the bodies that were found here on the island."

"That's what Gale and I thought. We chose to refrain from talking about it with my mom there, but we all know there's no coincidence when I have a vision."

"Yes, and certainly not something we want to talk about on our wedding day or our honeymoon."

"That's right, so kick this car into fourth and get

us to the reception. Then we can make our travel plans to France. I absolutely can't wait to see where my grandfather lived. This is going to be a trip of a lifetime."

"I think we actually have a window of opportunity next month. I didn't realize how difficult it would be to get our schedules coordinated."

Marie kissed Cory's cheek and wiped off the remains of lipstick. "Let's remember it was more *your* schedule that was the problem, not mine. I should be able to have someone fill in for me at the vet clinic."

Cory pulled into the parking spot next to the cadet blue beach house and halted to a stop. The open veranda faced the ocean allowing their guests to receive a magnificent view. "We'll discuss later whose schedule is more difficult, for now, Mrs. Miller, we have a perfect day for a reception. So, let's meet our guests and get this party started."

"Yes, and I need to check on Bailey. It was great how the catering staff agreed to watch him during the ceremony. I just hope he wasn't under their feet when they put out the food. You know how he likes to beg for scraps." Marie smiled at Cory as he held her hand getting out of the car when she suddenly began to feel dizzy and clumsily leaned against him. "Oh wow, I'm getting an overwhelming feeling of grief. I keep hearing cries and I feel so much negative energy. I suspect there were a lot of deaths here by the ocean."

Cory propped Marie against the car and lifted her chin with his finger. "Are you going to be okay? Do you need to do some meditating before we head to the party? That usually helps you keep the spirits at a distance."

"No, I'm fine, really I am. I've asked my spirit

guides to clear them off." Marie took in a deep breath and slowly blew it out. "Okay, there I'm better. Let's go change into our party clothes. I'm so glad we decided to keep the reception casual."

"Are you sure you're okay?"

Marie stood up and kissed Cory hard on the lips and then slowly pulled away and winked. "I'm perfect, remember? Let's go. I need to get out of this dress and into my rhinestone flip-flops."

Cory laughed and in one swift movement lifted Marie into his arms and carried her across the parking lot. "I'm at your beck and call. I have a feeling I'll be using the code words potato salad very soon."

"I'm beginning to crave potato salad already." Marie giggled and nestled her head into his neck and took in the woody musk scent of his cologne as they headed toward the beach house.

Isabella Swanson cowered in the corner of her bedroom as her mother screamed out her name and shook her violently. She squeezed her legs tight against her chest and tried to drown out the sound of a slicing sword against her ears. The constant screams and howls echoed in her head as tears ran down her cheeks. In one fell swoop, she felt herself being jolted up against the wall and then suddenly landed hard on the floor. When she opened her eyes, the screams were gone, and the only sound came from her mother praying on her knees in the corner of the room.

MARIE SAT STRAIGHT UP in bed and began waving her arms in the air. "No, stop that. Get it away from me."

Cory carefully pulled Marie into his chest and lovingly stroked her hair as Bailey dropped his chin on the bed. "Marie, are you having a dream or a vision? Shhh, it's okay, I'm here."

Marie began to feel the calm as Cory rocked her back and forth. She slowly opened her eyes, and there sitting in front of her on the antique rocker was Myra. "Myra, you're here. Where have you been? Were you at the wedding? Did you see the same vision I did?"

Cory released Marie and began looking around the dark room of the beach house and then looked at Marie. "Okay, I don't see anything, of course, so hey Myra, how are you? We miss you. It's not the same doing our ghost investigations without you."

Marie smiled. "She said she's always here and goes with us on the investigations. She also said our ceremony was perfect and loved the music we had at the reception. She knew we played *Tequila* just for her."

"Of course, we play all requests." Cory leaned in and kissed Marie's cheek. "Do you need to be alone with Myra?"

"Oh no of course not, she's here for a reason for both of us, I can sense it." Marie stopped and tilted her head as she listened to Myra at a higher frequency. "She did see my vision of a sword in the air. And there seems to be a young girl involved, not quite sure what that means. Either this girl saw the same thing, or she's involved somehow with this horrific sword. She also saw those skeletons I saw before the wedding ceremony. Somehow, you're going to be pulled into all of this. Cory, she thinks there is going to be a correlation of the skeletons and the sword with death."

Cory jumped when his cell phone rang, and he clumsily placed it to his ear. "Yes Tom, I was asleep, very funny. No, you didn't interrupt anything. What could you possibly want at this hour? You're kidding? Okay yes, I'll see you there in thirty minutes. Don't touch anything."

Marie turned on the light and saw Cory's blank look as he placed the phone on the nightstand. "What's going on?"

"You're never going to believe this. Tom just said they found a body on Sullivan's beach tangled up in the oat grass." Cory stared at Marie and then at the empty rocker. "Marie, Myra, the body had no head."

Marie grabbed Cory's arm. "Oh, that's horrible, and by the way, Myra's gone. She left as soon as you answered the phone. There seems to be a lot of turmoil on the other side with what's going on here. Would you mind if I came along?"

"Are you sure you want to do that?"

"Yes, I feel I'm being pulled to go with you, but we'll need to be quiet. We don't want to wake anyone."

"With as much as Gale and Tim drank, I highly doubt they're going to hear us. We need to be sure we don't wake your folks." Cory slipped on his khaki shorts and turned toward Marie. "I guess you were right about your vision. It's never a coincidence."

Marie got out of bed and began to get dressed. "No, it never is, and there must be some danger for Myra to have shown up right before that call. I think

I'm going to try and clear my head while we drive, we're going to need all the help we can get."

"I wouldn't say no to that." Cory grabbed his wallet and keys and quietly opened the bedroom door and whispered, "Well Mrs. Miller, it's our first case together as man and wife. Are you up for it?"

"More than you'll ever know." Marie hooked Bailey's leash on his collar as they quietly followed Cory out the door and down the stairs. "We can call Gale and Tim later and come back for our things."

"Okay, depending on how long this takes, we may miss the eleven o'clock brunch."

"That's okay, considering the circumstances, I think everyone will understand." Marie opened the door of the MG and guided Bailey into the tiny back seat and secured him to the safety harness. "Alright, let's roll."

Cory smiled at Marie as he buckled the retrofitted seatbelt and backed out of the parking lot. "There's one thing I won't deny. Life is never boring with you around."

"No, and the same goes for you, Chief Miller."

Marie allowed the warm night air to blow the cobwebs from her brain. She closed her eyes and began to call on her spirit guides for guidance. What her latest vision meant was uncertain, but she knew they were going to need more than the white light of protection. Beheaded bodies and sword's slicing through the air was a violent combination.

TWO

MARIE UNLEASHED Bailey from the harness and opened the door for him to stretch his legs from the cramped back seat. The multi-colored flashing police and ambulance lights created an odd glow over his chocolate fur. She cautioned him to remain at her side as she watched her husband gather information from his deputy.

A small smile fell on her face as she realized the chief of Sullivan's Island Police Department was her husband. The last three and a half years swiftly flashed before her eyes and made her realize how fortunate she was to have Cory in her life, along with her ever-faithful Labrador. Not to mention her dear friends and companions of the Sullivan's Island Paranormal Society. The SIPS team had done some pretty amazing things over the last few years. They've helped so many families with ghost investigations and coming to terms with their homes or businesses being haunted. Plus, their phenomenal talents that contributed to solving major crimes. It was so gratifying and very rewarding, but that was just the tip of the iceberg. These events would have never developed if she hadn't accepted her psychic ability as a gift and how her mentor, Myra Cummings, gave her the self-confidence to realize that fact. Her thoughts immediately drifted to Myra as a tear began to slip down her cheek and she quickly wiped it away when Cory approached her with a grim look on his face.

She said, "I gather you're not going to make it to brunch at the beach house."

"I'm not really sure." He reached down, patted Bailey on the back, then leaned against the car. "Marie, I can't even begin to describe what I just saw. Not what I had in mind for our wedding night. I'm going to have a ton of paperwork to take care of back at the station. I suggest you head back to our guests and try to sneak in a few hours of sleep."

"Actually, I may just go back to my place, I mean *our* place and sleep. I can call Mom and Gale and head back for brunch." She leaned forward and kissed Cory's nose. "I wish you could come back with me. It was exciting to watch you take charge of everything."

Cory smiled and pulled her tight against his chest. "We'll have plenty of time to make up for it, I promise."

Marie caught Tom Simmons approaching them out of the corner of her eye. "Maybe we should refrain from close contact until later. I wouldn't want you to lose face in front of your deputy."

Cory glanced over at Tom and asked, "What's up deputy?"

Tom rubbed the back of his neck as his radio bounced against his slender hips. He looked more like a senior in high school with his baby face, blonde hair, and fair skin. He was John Mullican's replacement, which naturally sent Marie back to the nightmare of

John murdering several women on the island before taking revenge on her with a rope around her neck.

"Sir, we got a match from IAFIS. The victim's name is Stephen Skerrett, and he was released six months ago from a federal prison in Estill for counter-feiting."

Cory asked, "Any other priors?"

"Nope, he was sentenced for counterfeiting money and other documents. He served fifteen years."

"What type of documents?" Marie asked catching Tom's side-glance. "Sorry, natural curiosity."

Tom smiled and said, "It looks like some legal and historical documents."

"Why on earth would someone cut off his head for counterfeiting? That sounds pretty extreme to me." Marie rubbed Bailey's head. "Unless he did a lousy job at it. "

"I guess that's what we'll need to find out. Tom, I need you to get the case files on our Mr. Skerrett and see who else may have known or been involved with him and his illegal activities. Somebody wasn't happy with his work and we'll need to line up interviews. I'll go to the morgue and get the findings on what it was that sliced his head off with such precision."

Marie shuddered and opened the car door and guided Bailey back into his harness. "I'm going to take Bailey home and get a few more hours of sleep. Keep in touch and let me know when you'll be free. We have wedding gifts to open, remember?"

Tom sheepishly said, "Congratulations and all. Sorry I didn't make it to the reception. Duty calls."

"That's fine, and thank you, Tom."

Cory followed Marie to the driver's side and

kissed her on the cheek. "I'll call you as soon as I can get free. Not sure how long this will take, but I promise to wrap it up as soon as possible. Get some sleep, okay?"

"I will, but I think we both know there's more to all of this than just a dead counterfeiter. Myra didn't show up for nothing." Marie got behind the wheel and started the vintage engine. "I'll see you soon, and I love you."

"Love you too Mrs. Miller." Cory tapped on the door and walked back over to the scurry of emergency vehicles.

Marie watched Cory through the rearview mirror and smiled as Bailey popped his head up to let the wind catch his snout. Life certainly wasn't dull being married to the chief of police, let alone being able to talk to the dead.

The peaceful sound of the ocean waves echoed as she pulled into her driveway. She unleashed Bailey to let him do his business and began to shuffle for her house key. Within a few seconds, a sharp pain shot through her neck as she stumbled against the palm tree and her head began to spin. A strange odor filled her nostrils and odd laughter clamored in her head. She couldn't handle the chaotic frenzy, so she cupped her hands over her ears and yelled out into the night air.

Marie awoke to Bailey licking her face and realized she was lying on her back staring up at the sky. "Bailey, how long was I out?"

Bailey wagged his tail and placed his paw on her arm. Marie looked at her watch and realized she had lain there for twenty minutes. She got up and brushed herself off and continued the search for her key and then placed it in the lock. She was thankful to be back on her own turf and quickly brushed her teeth, discarded her clothes, and then plunged face first down into the bed. Bailey jumped up and plowed his backside against her as she slowly drifted off to sleep.

AGAIN, Cory found himself in the cold, stark surroundings of the morgue staring at a pale grey lifeless body...only this one had no head. Murder never takes a day off, even for his wedding. He looked at his watch and hoped he'd be able to gather enough information to satisfy his duties and meet his wife, family, and friends for brunch.

He glanced up at Dr. Sally Brasher entering the morgue, the recently hired medical examiner, with a coffee in one hand, a medical chart in the other, and a pair of reading glasses on the top of her head hidden amongst her auburn mussed hair.

She took a sip of coffee and set it at the empty space above the shoulders on the silver metal table. "Hello Chief Miller, it looks like I get to match the face with the voice. We've talked so many times over the phone, glad to finally meet you in person."

Cory reached out and met her tiny latex covered hand and shook it. "Yes, nice to meet you. Sorry I haven't had the chance to meet you earlier. It's been a bit hectic lately."

"Yes, congratulations. I heard you got hitched. Wasn't that recent?" She slipped her glasses to the end of her nose and began to thumb through her papers.

"Yes, yesterday. In fact, I hope to get through this quickly, I have a brunch I need to attend."

Sally casually glanced up over her glasses and smiled. "Of course, I'll do the best that I can, but I hope you realize I do things a bit differently than Sue Patterson did. Not that there's anything wrong with the way she ran the office, but I like to do things in my own way, and that way is being thorough."

Cory sensed the tone in her voice and decided not to flex his muscles...yet. He gave his attention back to the body, which reminded him of a scene from *Sleepy Hollow*. "Of course, I apologize. So, what is it you've found to this point?"

Sally placed the charts on a side counter and pulled the white cotton sheet down to the waist of the headless body. "The time of death is uncertain at this point, but I'm going to venture a guess of about two weeks. I'll confirm that after the autopsy. As you can see, he was clearly into tattoos and must have gotten into a lot of fights because there are scars from knife wounds on his chest, sides, and both arms."

"He's certainly seen a lot of action for a counterfeiter." Cory stared at one of the tattoos and asked, "Are those tattooed dots on his hands?"

"Yes, I believe they represent the amount of time done in prison. You see these four dots on the outside? That's supposed to represent the four walls. And this dot here, between the thumb and forefinger, this one signifies when he entered prison and this one here means when he got out."

Cory glanced up and said, "You *are* very thorough. How do you know so much about tattoos?"

"I spent twenty years in New York and when you've been cutting into bodies as long as I have in a large city, you're bound to learn about tattoos." She grabbed the left shoulder and rolled the body on its side. "He's also got a few wounds on his back. This large scar is another knife wound, and this one here is from a bullet. So, this guy has been around the block before getting his head sliced off."

"Speaking of which, are you able to tell what type of knife or tool was used to make such a clean cut?"

"I'm still looking into that, but it would have to be something strong enough to have the power to chop off the head, as well as being very sharp."

Cory remembered Marie's vision and asked, "Possibly a sword?"

Sally raised her eyebrows and then narrowed her eyes. "Yes, I suppose a sword could easily cut off a head. What made you suspect a sword?"

"Let's just say I like being thorough also."

Sally smiled and said, "Good, then we should get along just fine."

THE RINGING WOULDN'T STOP as Marie tossed her head and rolled over on her side. She slowly opened her eyes and squinted at the sun when she realized the ringing was her phone. She slapped her hand on the nightstand and nearly knocked over the lamp and lazily placed the cell phone to her ear.

"Hello, yes this is Marie. No, no you didn't wake me." She rolled her eyes and tried to reposition herself out from under Bailey and shifted her elbow from his side. "Yes Mrs. Swanson, I remember you. Isabella is your daughter, correct? Okay, let me grab a pen and paper to write this down."

She began to write down the information and stopped in mid pen stroke. "Did you say the sound of a sword? Okay, I'll get back to you as soon as I can. I have a few things I need to do today, but I'll be able to talk with the SIPS team very soon. Thank you, and please give my best to Isabella."

Marie glanced at the clock and decided to get a quick shower and head back to Folly Island. She would be there just in time for their eleven o'clock brunch. When she glanced back at her notes, she circled the word sword and added a question mark when Bailey nudged her hand. "Okay boy, I'll let you out and then we're off for another ride. But you're going to have to get used to sleeping on the floor because there just isn't enough room in this bed for the two of us, let alone adding another person."

Marie took a quick glance in the mirror as she ran a brush through her wet hair. Bailey lapped up the last of his dog food and sloppily drank from his water bowl. She smiled at the mess he made on the floor and patted her thigh. "Come on buddy, let's go. It looks like we have another investigation with an added twist."

After the thirty-minute ride to Folly Island, Marie parked the car and then jogged up the back stairs to the veranda where the aroma of bacon and cinnamon caused her stomach to pang. The ocean breeze caught her face as Bailey ran ahead of her and straight into Mimi Rawlings stubby arms.

Marie chuckled and said, "Hey everyone, how are you all doing?"

Helen turned around and smiled. "We wondered when you would come down. We didn't want to interrupt anything. Where's Cory?"

Gale giggled and popped a strawberry into her mouth. "She probably wore him out."

"Very funny, actually he's not here. Both of us

weren't here for most of the night. He got a call for a case back on the island and I decided to go with him. Then I stayed at the house to get a few hours of sleep. He just sent me a text. He should be here shortly."

"What kind of case?" Jim Rawlings, Mimi's husband, carefully balanced the food on his plate as he plopped a spoon of scrambled eggs next to a stack of pancakes. His tall, thin frame showed no signs of overeating as his reddened scalp peered out from under his thinning hair. He claimed his lean build was from drinking too much coffee, which he did in excess due to the stress of being the owner of the Kangaroo Express on Middle Street on Sullivan's Island.

"We can discuss that later. Not really something we can talk about while we eat." Marie accepted a mimosa from Gale and asked, "How is your head feeling this morning?"

"It feels better now that I have a mimosa. Are you really going to wait to talk about *this* case, or are you trying to avoid the details for your parent's sake?"

"Yes to both questions, but I can share with you that it definitely ties in with my vision. Plus, Myra paid a visit to us right before Cory got the call. She saw the same headless skeletons."

"I knew it. I knew there would be more involved with this."

"What I'd like to share with the team is the phone call I received a little while ago. I'll wait until after we open our gifts and we're alone." Marie walked over to the buffet and stared in disbelief at the rows of bacon, scrambled eggs, French toast, waffles, fruit, fried green tomatoes, and a vast array of breads and muffins. "There's enough food here to feed everyone on Folly Island."

Marie filled her plate, sat beside Harry, chuckled at his usual rumpled attire, and taped up dark-rimmed glasses. She just knew he received heckles from the high school students, which was sad because he was an amazing counselor. Not to mention a thorough demonologist for their team. "Harry, how are you? Did you enjoy yourself at the wedding?"

Harry continued to stare at his plate and said, "Yes I did, and thank you for inviting me."

"We wouldn't have had it any other way. You know that. I'd like to share with you and the team about an investigation that involves a possible possession. Do you remember Mrs. Caroline Swanson? She lives in the condominium building on Middle Street across from the park."

"Oh yes, I know her. She's single and has two children. I've dealt with her son, Adam. He's a freshman and has been in quite a bit of trouble lately. I don't know a lot about the daughter."

"The daughter's name is Isabella, and that's what this investigation is about. Mrs. Swanson said she feels she's possessed. It should be interesting."

Gale sat next to Marie and glanced at Mimi's plate. "Mimi, are you on another diet? Your plate is full of healthy food."

"Yes, I am, but this one isn't any of those crazy crash diets. They never work for me. I've hired a nutritionist and she's helping me learn to eat the right foods. I met her when she came into the pharmacy a few months ago. It seems to be working because I'm never hungry and I've lost seven pounds already." She bit into a piece of pineapple and smiled with pride. Her salt and pepper crimped curls fell tight against her scalp and the once plump dimples in her cheeks appeared to be less concave due to the weight loss. As the pharmacist and owner of the local pharmacy on Sullivan's Island, Mimi was exposed to many crazy diet fads.

"I think that's great Mimi." Tim Haines plopped his packed plate of food on the table next to Gale and sat down. He reached for a roll exposing his muscular biceps through his fire chief T-shirt.

"You may need a nutritionist soon if you keep eating like that." Gale winked and then stole a teetering piece of bacon off the top of his waffles and grits.

Marie chuckled and slipped a piece of wheat toast to Bailey. She stood up as soon as she saw Cory come up the stairs and motioned for him to sit next to her. "Now that Cory is here, we'd like to thank everyone for coming and being a part of our special day. It was perfect in every way. Mom and Dad, thank you for all that you've done, we couldn't be more grateful. Taking the burden out of the planning was a huge help. To Gale and Tim, thank you for all of your help and the great bachelor and bachelorette parties. Of course, those details will remain classified."

Cory laughed and said, "I'd also like to thank my cousin Erica for allowing us to use this amazing place for the reception. And a huge thank you to the staff and the amazing food we've had over the last two days."

Marie smiled at the cheers and laughter and sat back down. "Cory why don't you get some food and then you can fill me in on what, if anything, you learned from the medical examiner."

"I need coffee more than anything. I didn't get much sleep. I wanted to finish as much paperwork as

I could so I wouldn't miss this." He kissed Marie's nose and headed over to the buffet table.

Marie smiled at her father and brothers and held up her mimosa in a private toast and then continued eating her eggs. She glanced around the table and smiled with pleasure and contentment with having so many wonderful people in her life, but she still wasn't able to fill the void from the loss of Myra, no matter how hard she tried.

Everyone sauntered into the main living room after brunch and shared in the opening of the wedding gifts. Many oohs and aahs were exchanged as Gale noted which gifts came from whom. Helen and Paul made their excuses to finish packing, along with her brothers, as friends said their goodbyes leaving Marie, Cory, and the SIPS team alone.

Gale tightened the scrunchy around her coal black ponytail and finished the last drop of her mimosa. "Well then, why don't you fill us in on this phone call you received this morning, and then Cory can tell us about his case."

"Alright, first I want to let you all know that I had a very strange vision right before the wedding yesterday about some headless skeletons on the beach. Gale and I wondered if it tied in with the bodies they found here back in nineteen eighty-seven."

Harry adjusted his dark-rimmed glasses and fidgeted with his bow tie. "Do you think it was just your psychic abilities homing in on those bodies, or was it something else?"

"Not sure, but right before Cory received the call for this case, Myra paid us a visit and she too knew about the bodies. We all know that wasn't a fluke."

Mimi rubbed Bailey's back and sheepishly asked, "How is Myra? Is she here with us now?"

Marie smiled and said, "She's great I guess, and no she isn't here right now. But I'm sure she'll turn up when she's needed."

Tim stretched his back and leaned further into the plush settee. "By the way, I'm not sure I know the actual history of those bodies that were found here."

Harry replied, "In May of nineteen eighty-seven, fourteen bodies were found while excavating a construction site at the west end of Folly Beach. They stopped construction for a month while the South Carolina Institute of Archeology and Anthropology investigated the remains. All of the bodies, except one, had been buried with shoulders directed to the west. Twelve of the bodies were missing skulls and other major body parts. Some of them had coffins. Others only had ponchos. They also found Union Army Eagle buttons, an Enfield rifle, and some mini balls. It was decided the men were from the Union Army's Fifty-Fifth Massachusetts Volunteer Regiment that was in this area during the Civil War. They had no injuries, so the possibility of death in battle was eliminated. That left the possibility of death by illness, head injury or beheading. There are several unconfirmed opinions as to why the remains were minus skulls. One theory is that bounty hunters sought the skulls of buried Union soldiers when the Federal government offered rewards for the retrieval of bodies. But oddly, while the skulls were missing, the rest of the bones were undisturbed, and the bodies were either reburied or originally buried without heads.

Jim said, "And it's not likely bounty hunters would be so respectful when *collecting* their prizes."

"Exactly, and another opinion was that the skulls were removed by local islanders for voodoo rituals, which I find to be far-fetched. There were other equally scary opinions offered, but this is one mystery that may never be solved." Harry removed his glasses and wiped the lens with his stained vest.

"That could be a great place to do an investigation." Marie smiled and continued, "I'm going to let Cory fill us in on what his case is all about and then I can share with you the phone call I received from Mrs. Swanson."

Cory finished his coffee and set the cup on the walnut side table. "I got a call from Tom that they found a body entangled in the oat grass at the edge of the beach on Sullivan's Island. It appears the body had been beheaded."

"Wow, are you serious? Did you find the head?" Jim sat up in the chocolate leather high back wing chair.

"No, actually we didn't. Dr. Brasher's autopsy showed that the head was cut off with something very sharp and strong."

Jim asked, "Isn't Sally Brasher the new medical examiner? They say she's sort of a tight ass."

Mimi rolled her eyes. "Just because a woman does her job well doesn't mean she's a tight ass."

Marie raised her eyebrow and said, "I'm not sure about her tight ass but this may tie in with my vision of a sword, along with Isabella Swanson hearing a sword slice through the air when her mother claims she was possessed, but I'll explain more on that later."

Cory continued, "The victim's name is Stephen

Skerrett, and he was in federal prison for counterfeiting. The strange thing I learned from examining our victim was that he had knife wounds all over his body, along with a gunshot wound and a ton of tattoos. He seems to have had a lot of action that involved more than counterfeiting. That's all I have for now."

"What I wanted to run by all of you is the phone call from Mrs. Caroline Swanson about her daughter, Isabella." Marie shifted in her seat and uncrossed her slender tanned legs. "Over the last couple of months, Isabella has been waking up in the middle of the night screaming that she hears voices and ringing in her ears. The voices have gotten more frequent, which has caused her to miss a lot of school and taken her on frequent trips to doctors and psychiatrists. They haven't been able to diagnose her with anything, which has led Mrs. Swanson to believe Isabella is possessed."

"What an awful thing to have happened to someone so young." Mimi crossed her arms over her stout breast.

"Yes, well Mrs. Swanson also stated they'd noticed strange noises coming from their attic. She said it sounds like groaning and footsteps up and down the stairway. Her son has admitted to the same noises." Marie glanced at Harry. "This makes sense with what Harry mentioned to me earlier that Adam has been getting into more trouble over the last few months."

"So, what does Mrs. Swanson want us to do?" Gale placed the notebook that was on her lap onto the walnut coffee table and longingly stared at the empty mimosa glass.

"She asked us to do an investigation and help her daughter. She wants us to do an exorcism and I explained to her that isn't something we commonly do, but that Harry may be able to help her out." Marie leaned forward and placed her elbows on her knees. "The thing is I'm not so sure she's possessed."

Gale asked, "Why do you say that?"

"Because the symptoms that Mrs. Swanson described reminded me of what I went through when I was her age. I think Isabella is showing signs of being psychic."

THREE

ISABELLA SAT in the courtyard outside her condo building and stared at her cup of tea. Marie noticed the dark circles under her eyes and her tangled dishwater blonde hair. Her shoulders were slumped over the concrete table and her pale skin gleamed in the sun.

Marie cautiously sat next to Isabella and pulled a stray strand of hair from her cheek and tucked it behind her ear. "Hello Isabella, my name is Marie. Your mom called us here to help with what's been going on in your home. Can you share with me what you've been experiencing?"

Isabella continued to stare at the steaming tea and replied, "I'm a freak."

Marie choked back the tears and said, "Isabella, you most certainly are not a freak."

Isabella slowly raised her head and stared into Marie's eyes. "Oh yeah, then who's the little old woman sitting next to you?"

Marie smiled, "Why I'm going to go out on a limb and say that her name is Myra Cummings and she's my mentor and best friend. She was a member of the

SIPS team and now my spirit guide. I've got a few others too."

Isabella continued to stare at Marie as a slow smile began to form at the corners of her mouth. "You mean to tell me that you see her too? And the others that are around you?"

"Of course I do, and the reason you do is that I believe you have some psychic ability. And that's what I'm here to help you with. We all are." Marie felt a warm breeze against her face and continued, "Isabella, I too had the same experiences when I was your age. How old are you now?"

"I just turned thirteen last Saturday."

"What exactly are you experiencing and when did it begin?"

"I can see and hear dead people all the time. I think the first time it happened was when my grandmother died. I was four. I remember seeing her as plain as day and I felt all warm and happy. She told me everything was going to be alright and anytime I'm frightened by another dead person, she comes around." Isabella sat up and wiped a tear from her cheek. "Is she my spirit guide?"

"She certainly is, and I can see her right now. She's standing right behind you."

"Yeah, I can feel her. It's a completely different feeling than what I felt the other night."

"I'd like for you to try and explain to me what it was you experienced the other night. I know your mom was terrified."

Isabella shivered and began to rub her arms. "It was one of the scariest things I've ever had happen to me. I woke up to a loud scream in my head. It echoed in my ears and I could feel this terrible pain in my neck. I couldn't get the scream to stop and then there was this strange sound that I can only describe it from the movie *Pirates of the Caribbean*. You know when Johnny Depp gets into a sword fight."

"Myra and I had the same vision. Isabella, you're not crazy or possessed. You have been blessed with a gift, although I know right now you don't feel as if it's a gift. I didn't either when I was your age. In fact, I tried to squelch it until a few years ago, and it's not healthy. But I'd like to help you through this if you'll let me. There are many tools you can use to control your ability and to keep the spirits at arm's length."

"Really, you can help me?"

"Of course I can. Between your grandmother, Myra, and me, we'll be able to stop the horrible anxiety and night terrors."

Isabella smiled wide for the first time during their conversation and said, "Thank you. You're the first person to believe me. I've been to so many doctors and have had more needles stuck in me over the last several months than you can imagine."

"I think I understand." Marie grabbed her hand and said, "Why don't you come inside and help the SIPS team set up for the investigation? Would you like to take part and use some of the equipment? I think it may help you gain some confidence in your ability."

"Oh cool, I'd love that. I watch all the ghost investigation shows. I've always wanted to go on a ghost hunt."

"Great, then why don't you come with me and I'll introduce you to the team."

"For the first time since this all started, I feel relaxed." Isabella tightly wrapped her arms around

Marie's waist. "Thank you for believing in me. I've never been able to share any of this with my friends. My best friend Connie freaked out when I told her and hasn't talked to me in six months. Her mother won't let her play with me anymore. I was actually beginning to think I *was* crazy or possessed."

Marie's heart skipped a beat as she cupped Isabella's chin in her hand. "You're not crazy Isabella. You're a psychic and I'm going to help you learn how amazing it is and how to embrace the gift you've been given."

They both walked toward the condominium with their arms wrapped around each other. Marie felt a huge sense of pride and accomplishment as she gave a wink to Myra who waited for them at the edge of Isabella's screen door.

JACKSON TYLER GRUMBLED as he pulled his red wagon stuffed with piles of garbage bags over to the dumpsters behind their apartment complex. His mother nagged him for an hour to help clean the storage unit before he was allowed to do any fishing with his buddies. They'd already been at it for two hours and he just knew he was missing out on some of the best fishing of the day, especially now with the light rain beginning to fall.

He stopped his wagon at the edge of the smelly green dumpster and dragged a concrete block that was lying on the other side of the lot to the edge of the bin. He stepped up on the block and shoved the lid up off the top and winced at the pungent stench emanating from inside. He carefully gripped the first plastic bag and heaved it inside and grabbed the frame to keep from losing his balance. As he bent down to grab the next bag, he noticed his hands were covered with a red sticky substance.

He wiped them off on the bag, but his curiosity got the best of him as he placed both hands on the frame of the dumpster and slowly pulled himself up to look inside. There staring back at him were maggot filled eye sockets and what appeared to be the remains of a head.

He screamed and fell back onto the ground landing on his side as he frantically grabbed the wagon handle and ran back to his apartment screaming for his mother to call the police and tell them there was a half-eaten head lying in the dumpster.

ISABELLA WATCHED with curiosity and excitement as the SIPS team began to unload their equipment and place cameras in certain corners of their condominium. She was annoyed that her brother Adam, a tall, lanky freshman with long brown hair tied into a ponytail, was helping tape down the extension cords. In order to prove herself, she decided to push her way through the group and lend them a hand.

Marie caught Isabella standing next to her and asked, "Would you mind carrying that case over there and follow me into your kitchen? I think we're going to make that command central."

"Command central, what does that mean?"

"We usually pick a room that doesn't have any spirit activity and set up our computers so we can view all of the camera angles. If we can't find a room to use, we set up outside in one of our vehicles."

Isabella helped Marie set the case on the kitchen island. "Wow, I had no idea how much was involved to do an investigation. You don't normally see all of that on those ghost investigation shows."

"Yeah, they normally only have forty minutes of actual show time. They don't illustrate how much time is spent interviewing the client, researching the history of the location, and then placing all of the equipment in the right spots." Marie began to plug in the laptop. "Let alone the number of hours spent going over the analysis. Any good investigative team will spend a minimum of two weeks to do a proper investigation. Some investigations can go on for a year. Our main goal is to be sure every client is satisfied with the results."

"How do you squeeze all of this in and then help all the animals at the animal hospital?"

"That's a good question, Isabella. It does keep me going in all directions, but I love being a vet, as well as a ghost investigator." Marie typed in the computer password and winked at Isabella. "Not to mention being a psychic medium. I guess all three of these areas have me helping others in some capacity, which gives me a lot of peace."

"I hope I can be just like you and help others with whatever psychic abilities I may have."

Marie finished synching the camera positions on the main twenty-seven-inch screen and smiled at Isabella. "I think that's a great attitude to have and I'm going to do everything I can to teach you how to control your ability. There are some great tools that Myra taught me that I'd like to pass onto you that should help you tell the spirits when you're ready to help, and when you're not."

Gale walked into the kitchen with a KII meter in one hand and an LED flashlight in the other. "Are there any batteries in that case? I need to replace them for this flashlight. I think we're about finished setting everything up. Harry has some notes from Isabella's mom on where most of the activity has taken place."

"Great, I'm going to have Isabella with you and me, if you don't mind. I want her to get a feel for any areas that she's being drawn to, as well as if she can pick up on anything."

Gale winked at Isabella. "That works for me. We're more fun than anyone else anyway."

Isabella laughed and said, "You have great hair. My brother talks about you all of the time. Only I don't think he's interested in your hair."

Marie rolled her eyes. "Don't tell her anymore Isabella. We have a hard enough time getting her head through the doors."

"Very funny and thank you for the compliment on my hair. That was very kind of you. I work hard to look this good."

Tim walked into the kitchen and immediately turned around and held up his hand toward Gale. "This isn't a conversation I want to be involved in."

Gale turned on her heels and pulled on the back of his shirt. "But why honey, you know you love the way I look."

Marie shook her head at Isabella. "We try not to encourage her."

Isabella laughed and followed Marie into the living room. The team gathered in a circle as Marie asked everyone to close their eyes and envision a white circle of white light around their bodies. They repeated the protection prayer and broke out into groups of two. Harry and Jim were at command central; Tim and Mimi were first on the investigation doing electromagnetic field readings inside the condominium, while Marie, Gale, and Isabella went outside and sat down at the concrete table. Marie pulled out a small candle and placed it in the middle of the table while Gale lit it with her lighter.

Marie looked at Isabella and said, "I want you to close your eyes and take in long slow deep breaths through your nose, and then slowly blow out through your mouth. As you release each breath, I want you to try and clear your mind and tell me what you feel. Is there any place here that you are being drawn to?"

With her eyes closed, Isabella said, "I'm being drawn to my bedroom."

"Alright, then that's where we will go. In the meantime, in order for you to stay focused on this particular area, you need to try and shut out any other disturbances from spirit by picturing a closed door at the top of your head. Actually, envision a door closing and it'll quiet all of those voices you hear in your head."

"Hey, it's starting to work." Isabella gave Marie a big smile and followed her and Gale into the condominium.

CORY OBSERVED the forensics team carefully place the rotting head onto the plastic tarp on the ground as Sally slipped on her latex gloves. A team member continued to take pictures and gave the okay for Sally to examine the head. She carefully assessed the severed neck and proceeded to inspect the back of the head.

"I didn't think medical examiners came on the scene for a body part." Cory crouched down next to Sally and winced at the putrid odor of rotting flesh.

Sally placed the head back on the tarp and said, "I normally don't, but my curiosity got the best of me. I had a hunch, and after a closer look, I'm certain this head matches up with our body in the morgue."

"I think I agree with that hunch. Does the time-frame of death match that of the body?"

"It's hard to say exactly because the head has more decomposition from the heat of being in the dumpster, but I'd say yeah, it's a match. The way the head was sliced at the neck also matches the body. I'll send my report when I'm finished."

Cory stood back up and pointed at Jackson. "Is he our witness?"

Sally squinted from the setting sun and looked at the boy. "Yeah, I think he gave his statement to one of the officers on the scene. He was pretty freaked out. Can't blame him; not a normal thing to find in a dumpster."

Cory shook his head. "Yeah, well I'd better go talk with him. Thanks for the information and I'll look for your report. I'm going to need a little more to go on to proceed with the investigation."

Sally stood up and removed her gloves. "I would imagine finding any witness is going to be difficult."

Cory walked toward the boy wearing a raincoat sitting on the curb next to his mother and ran through his mind how to approach him for questioning. This wasn't the time to be all business and matter of fact. Just because he was able to shut out the gory details, didn't mean a ten-year-old could do it. No, this was one of the sides to the job he wished he wasn't a part of, along with telling a loved one someone was dead. He tipped back his hat, gathered his thoughts, and sat down next to Jackson instantly wishing he was back at the beach house with Marie.

ISABELLA SAT with Marie on her bed and pointed toward the closet. "The dark shadow stays in the closet when I'm not alone."

Marie could feel the presence but continued to take EMF readings. "Does the shadow come out when you're by yourself?"

"Sometimes it will, but more often when I'm trying to sleep." Isabella looked at the instrument Marie was holding and asked, "What is that thing?"

Marie replied, "It's an electromagnetic field detector. We use it to measure electromagnetic fields or EMF for short. Basically, it picks up an electrical surge in an area that sometimes can be as simple as an electric cord plugged into the wall. If there's no presence of any cable wires or electronics, it's possible it's the energy coming from a spirit trying to manifest itself."

Gale held out the digital voice recorder and said, "Is there anyone here with us? If so, we'd love to talk with you. You can talk right into this recorder. We just want to know why you are here and why you're scaring Isabella and her family."

Isabella jumped and grabbed Marie's hand. "It's right next to Gale. It's a little boy, can you see him?"

Marie said, "Yes I can, and you're doing great Isabella. You can ask him questions with your mind, which is called telepathy. Don't be afraid. You need to work through that fear. See if you can find out what he wants and if you can help him."

Isabella closed her eyes for a moment and said, "He's trying to find his family. He's lost."

"We can try to help him. I want you to calm him with your thoughts. Reassure him that he needs to go through the light and that his family is waiting for him. We'll both tell him. We can do this together."

"I can see his family." Isabella smiled and after a few moments she opened her eyes and looked at Marie. "He crossed over. That was amazing. I feel so calm. I could feel how happy he was to finally find his family."

"Yes, that's exactly how I feel when I've helped someone cross over. You see there wasn't anything to be afraid of. When you are able to control how the spirits approach you, you'll soon learn to help them individually."

"Can you please share this with my mother? I know she's frightened and she needs to know I'm not possessed. I think she needs help understanding all of this too."

"I'd be happy to talk with her. We all will." Marie looked at Gale. "Maybe we can also set up an appointment with Cheryl."

"That's a great idea."

Isabella asked, "Who's that?"

"Cheryl Alexander is a doctor of parapsychology. Myra had me meet with her when I was first learning to understand my abilities. She's a great lady and would be able to work with you and your family on how to deal with all of this. I think it's important for all of you to discuss this with a professional. It'll help you and your family work through any fears or confusion." Marie stood up and turned off the EMF meter. "Come on, let's head back to command central and fill everyone in on what you did. I think we've got enough evidence to call it a night."

Gale followed Marie and Isabella out of the room. "Sounds good to me, I'm exhausted, gotta keep up with my beauty sleep."

Isabella whispered to Marie. "You were right. I can see why you don't pay her too many compliments."

Gale frowned and said, "Hey I heard that. That'll be enough out of the both of you."

FOUR

MARIE SAT across the table of local citizens of Sullivan's Island at the Carolina Day committee meeting. Myra had asked her to serve with this group three years ago and being back without her was another step of moving forward. She hoped to honor Myra in making this year's Carolina Day a success.

Gale grudgingly accepted Marie's invitation to serve on the committee and made her feelings known while staring across the room with a look of exasperation. She placed her smart phone on the table and began perusing her email and said, "How long do these meetings take?"

Marie sighed at Gale without taking her eyes off the head of the committee, Deidra Young, and whispered. "As long as needed, and would you kindly return your phone to your purse and pay attention to Deidra?"

"Deidra's a twit and you know it. She's like a Stepford wife on steroids," she whispered back. "Even Myra felt they needed some new blood to head this committee. Why don't you step up to the plate?

You'd do a great job at running this committee, and Myra would be honored."

"Don't even use Myra as a ploy to guilt me into running this thing. Not fair, and besides, Deidra's alright. We have enough of a committee to keep Carolina Day a success. She works well with the SC Historical Society." Marie casually grabbed Gale's phone and slipped it into her purse. "Now pay attention."

Gale rolled her eyes. "You're a real buzzkill, you know that?"

Marie glanced around the conference table and began to take in the members of the committee. Deidra was a high school teacher around forty-five and known as the island gossip. She had a good heart but couldn't refrain from sharing personal business about everyone. Her dyed red hair was held in place with layers of hairspray, and her makeup was impeccable. She dressed in the latest fashions and never left the house unless without her six-inch heels. Gale was right. She did look like a Stepford wife on steroids.

Cameron Letterbach, known as Cam, was a jolly fellow with plush gray hair and a matching mustache. He owned the Co-Op and always brought snacks to the meetings. He recently lost his wife, Betty, and lately looked lost. Even though he wore a smile on his face, it was apparent he missed his wife.

Genevieve Baxter was the librarian at the Edgar Allan Poe Library and also worked part-time at the Co-Op for Cam. She was an excellent source for doing the research for the committee and also helped Marie and the SIPS team on occasion. She exuded the stereotypical persona of a librarian with her mousy brown hair pulled back in a bun. Her voice was in a constant whisper, obviously due from years of working at the library.

Professor Dirk Cooper had perfectly coiffed brown hair and wore dark, vintage round-framed glasses. He had recently retired from the University of North Carolina and was the man responsible for substantial contributions to the community. He was the primary donor for Thompson Park, a small interpretive park at the Breach Inlet overlook on Sullivan's Island. His tall frame gave off an authoritative presence, but his calm nature left him unassuming and the least likely to have gobs of money.

Last, and of course not least, was the character of the committee, Cal Murray. Cal was a park ranger at Fort Moultrie and the island's historian. He had a salt and pepper beard and mustache, and his fun nature usually left the group in stitches more often than not. But all kidding aside, his wealth of knowledge about the history of Sullivan's Island, and everything there was to know that took place at the fort made him the go-to guy for anything involving history.

Marie felt Gale's elbow in her side and said, "What?"

Gale chuckled and pulled her phone back out of Marie's purse. "Now look at who's not paying attention. Deidra just asked if you'd be willing to do psychic readings the way Myra used to do for the fundraiser."

Marie sheepishly looked at Deidra and smiled. "Sorry, I guess I was daydreaming. I suppose I could do some readings. I've never actually done that before. I can still donate my usual free vet check-up if you wish. Let me get back to you on the readings."

Deidra replied, "That would be fine. Let us know.

I remember Myra was able to bring in quite a bit of money for us."

After all the notes had been taken on certain required responsibilities, the meeting adjourned and Marie and Gale found themselves walking back to their houses on the beach. Marie and Gale's friendship had become better than sister-like, and Marie couldn't imagine life without Gale in it. Not only was she her best friend, but, also, she was the yin to her yang, or so a psychic in New Orleans told them.

Gale ran the local antique shop in the front room of her beach house, and it was quite convenient for her living three doors down from Marie. Since Cory moved in with Marie, Gale made a promise to give a courtesy call before she dropped in unannounced. This was decided after Gale had walked in on the couple in the living room in a compromising position.

Gale removed her sandals as soon as her feet hit the sand and plopped them in her oversized turquoise purse. "Marie, are you going to do the readings for the fundraiser as Myra did?"

"I don't know. I've never actually done something like that, although I suppose I could. I'm still getting a grasp on organizing how the spirits come to me. There are times I have no control."

"By the way, were you having another vision when you faded out in the meeting or were you as bored as I was?"

Marie smiled and shook her head. "I had an idea that I want to run by you." Reaching her deck stairs, she walked up to the door and opened it for Bailey. As he continued to sniff for the perfect spot to relieve his bladder, Marie continued, "What would you think of turning Myra's place into a retreat for kids with psychic abilities?"

Gale cocked her head and asked, "How so?"

"After what we were able to do for Isabella, I started to think maybe we could create an environment to help other kids and their family members deal with understanding their psychic abilities. We could have Cheryl attend and help them talk about their fears, frustration, and any other confusing things going on in their lives. Help them to learn what it's like to be psychic or to have children that are psychic. Maybe we could turn it into a long weekend retreat. The SIPS team could help them do an investigation. You saw what it did for Isabella being involved and finally helping the little boy cross over."

"Marie, that's a fantastic idea. You've been struggling what to do with Myra's house after she left it to you. That could be where they stay. There's plenty of room. You could have a couple of families together. Maybe if they see other kids have the same ability, they won't feel like freaks, as Isabella so eloquently stated."

"That's even better. Wow, I really like where this is going." Marie pulled Bailey into her chest and kissed his head. "And maybe even Bailey can be of some help. Dogs are amazing for therapy, right?"

"How do you want to begin?"

"It'd be nice to help defray any travel costs for the family, so maybe we can use the money Myra left and expand on that. I don't want to turn this into another fundraiser, but there may be opportunities to increase the amount."

Gale pulled herself up from the stairs and began

stretching her legs. "Let's chat more about this tomorrow. I'm meeting Tim for a nightcap."

"Sounds like a plan. I hope Cory gets home soon. He texted me earlier that the head they found matches up with the body. What is the purpose of slicing someone's head off? I mean it's such a drastic way to kill someone, don't you think?"

"Tim said it sounded like revenge. I don't know, but I'm sure you'll be pulled into it even further. What I'd like to know is why Isabella had the vision of the sword. How does she tie into it?"

Marie shrugged her shoulders and said, "I don't know, I think Cheryl may be able to help more with that. I'm glad Isabella and her mom agreed to talk with her. It drives me crazy how these small snippets come and go with my visions. It's hard to place what they mean."

"You need to meditate. It helps you know. You've even got me doing it more now."

Marie chuckled, "Good I'm glad. I have a long day at the hospital tomorrow. I need to get some sleep. Take it easy, girlfriend, talk to you soon."

"Back at ya."

THE DEEP WHISPER of her name startled Isabella out of her sleep as she frantically looked around her room. Cautiously lifting her head off the pillow, she glanced at the ball of light dancing across the window from outside. As she slowly got out of bed to see where the light had gone, she again heard her name echo in her mind. Without realizing it, she telepathically called out to her grandmother and pictured a door closing at the top of her head. Her body relaxed as a warm breeze surrounded her and the silhouette of her grandmother appeared at the foot of her bed.

Isabella smiled and asked why her grandmother was there when a sudden slam of an outside door startled her. She ran out of her room and down the hall only to find her brother Adam standing frozen in the middle of the living room pointing to the window. When Isabella called for him, he slowly turned and wickedly whispered her name. Without thinking, she ran over to her brother and shook him until his eyes focused on her.

He asked, "Where am I? What am I doing in the middle of the living room?"

Isabella guided him to the couch and sat him down. "I don't know. I woke up out of my sleep by a creepy voice whispering my name. I saw a ball of light dancing outside my window, and I immediately did what Marie taught me to do and pictured a door closing at the top of my head. Just then I felt calm and saw grandma by my bed. Then I heard a door slam and came out here to find you standing like you were all crippled up and frozen pointing outside. Then you whispered my name in that same creepy voice."

Adam shook his head and lounged against the back of the couch. "All I remember was I felt like I was floating. I think I saw a ball of light too. Then I think I saw myself. Like it was a reflection of me, only I looked...like I was dead. The next thing I remember you were shaking me. Isabella, what's going on in this place? Why are all these things happening? How did you see grandma?"

"She's my spirit guide. She protects me. She probably protects you too." Isabella leaned forward and began to rub her arms warding off a chill. "Adam, I think I'd better call Marie again. I think we need her help. There's more going on than just the little boy I helped cross over to the other side. I wonder if the SIPS team came up with any evidence from their investigation here."

Adam rubbed his eyes and said, "I hope they did because this is all starting to freak me out."

"You and me both, Adam...you and me both."

MARIE QUICKLY LEFT the hospital at eleven a.m. and met the SIPS team in their meeting room above her garage. They sat around the conference table intently poring through mounds of evidence they recorded at Isabella's condo. After three hours, most of the footage caught showed no signs of spirit activity, but they still had a few hours of EVPs to review.

Marie removed her headphones and motioned for Gale to do the same. "I need you to listen to this. I'm going to take out some of the back noise and then tell me what you hear."

Gale stood up and placed the headphones over her ears and gave Marie the thumbs up. "Go for it." After twenty seconds, Gale's shoulders jerked and her eyes grew large as she ripped off the headphones and said, "It was someone crying for help."

"That's what I thought it said. It was faint in the background and it sounds like a male voice."

Gale placed the headphones back on. "Play it back again. Yeah, it's a male voice asking for help. Wow, what a catch."

"Let me mark it here and then we can have Harry place it on the final analysis recording. This is something to take back to Isabella. I think this is separate from the little boy we crossed over. Not sure what it means, but we can chat with her about it."

Harry wrote some notes on his tablet and called to Marie from the other end of the conference table. "Marie, I just caught something from the camera in the living room. It took place only seconds before we were wrapping up for the night. Come and take a look at this."

Marie, Gale, and the rest of the team stood behind Harry and watched the replay. Within a few seconds, they all saw a ball of light flash across the living room window from outside of the condo as a dark mist slithered across the floor and then shot out of the room.

"Okay, now that is very weird. What do you suppose that was?" Mimi rubbed her watering eyes from under her glasses. "I need to see that again. My eyes are tired from watching all of these recordings."

"Yes, Harry, please play that through again in slow motion." After careful review, Marie said, "Wait, stop it there. Gale, what's the time stamp on that? Right here when the black mist appears."

Gale squinted at the screen. "Two thirty-two point sixteen, why?"

Marie ran over to her notebook and brought it over to the group. "Look here, that's the exact time we heard the cry for help."

Jim plopped back down into his chair. "I think we all know there's a correlation between the light and cry for help."

Marie began to flip through her notes when her cell phone rang. She grabbed it off the table and said, "Hi Isabella, what can I do for you? He did? Is he okay? I see...a ball of light and a creepy voice. We are about done going through our evidence and we have something we just came across that could be very interesting, especially with what you just told me. Why don't you and Adam come over to my place this evening around eight? I think we should have a final analysis put together for you then. Yes, by all means, bring your mother along. We'd love for her to see this also. Yes, we'll see you then, goodbye."

Harry pushed the taped glasses up his nose and asked, "Did I hear you mention a ball of light?"

"You sure did, but I'm a little concerned about what Adam saw." Marie explained what took place at Isabella's place the night before and grabbed her notebook and pen. "I'm going to write all of this down. It certainly does match up with what we just caught on tape."

"Yeah, except for the cry for help. Not sure how any of that matches up." Tim took a swig of coffee from his mug and rubbed the back of his neck and asked, "What causes a ball of light like that anyway? Plus, what is with Adam seeing himself?"

Marie replied, "She said the ball of light was about the size of a baseball, which is what we saw on the tape. It's possible it was her grandmother. She's her spirit guide, or it could have been another spirit. The science field describes it as phosphenes or optic neuritis. They say it's a precursor to a severe migraine or seizure. But I think we all know this isn't the case. We saw the ball of light also."

Jim asked, "As far as Adam seeing himself, do you think it could be a doppelganger?"

Harry replied, "I've never heard or seen anything like that in my years of study and investigating. It's supposed to be folklore describing someone seeing a double of themselves and can bring them bad luck, or even death."

"I don't believe in any of that nonsense. I'm pretty open-minded on a lot of things in our field, but doppelganger, I'm not so sure." Mimi continued to rub Bailey's back with her foot.

Gale grabbed a cold piece of bacon and popped it in her mouth. "I'm not sure about that either, but we don't rule any of these things out. I think we need to finish up the audio so we can put all of this together for this evening."

Marie said, "I agree with Gale. I think we need to investigate further, maybe see if anyone has had this experience. Just because we've not experienced it, doesn't mean it isn't real."

Tim asked, "By the way Marie, what came back on the head that was found in the dumpster?"

"Cory said it was a match to the body they found. I'm having a hard time understanding all of this, but I do think there's a correlation with my vision of the headless skeletons. I just can't piece it together yet. Oh, and I also forgot to mention to everyone that Gale and I were thinking of turning Myra's place into a sort of retreat home for psychic kids. After what Isabella has been through, we thought there might be more kids out there who are afraid to admit what they're witnessing. Maybe include Cheryl Alexander also."

Gale added, "We also thought we could use some of the money Myra left to help defray the costs for kids and their families to travel here."

Mimi smiled and said, "I think that's an amazing idea. We could all help in some way. You saw how it helped Isabella being involved in the investigation.

Maybe we could include that in their therapy, along with Bailey here."

Jim nodded. "Yeah, make it a group effort, power and confidence in numbers."

"We thought we'd have two or three kids and maybe one of their parents here for a weekend. We can chat more about this later. But I'm so glad you're all on board with the idea." Marie looked at Harry and said, "Harry, you're kind of quiet. Would you like to be a part of this?"

Gale rolled her eyes and quickly said, "Oh, he just doesn't get along with Cheryl."

"That's not true. We just have differences of opinions." Harry looked at Marie. "I think it's a great idea and I'm on board."

Tim tipped his baseball hat back on his head exposing his brown, buzz cut hair. "Count me in."

"Great, then we have a plan. I'll contact Cheryl and see if she'd like to be a part of this, although I sort of doubt she'll say no. She loved Myra too. This will be a great tribute."

FIVE

MARIE PAID close attention to Isabella, Caroline and Adam's responses to the video and asked, "Is this what you saw last evening?"

Adam's eyes remained on the screen and nodded his head. "Yes, that's what I saw."

Isabella looked at Marie and then back at the screen. "I didn't hear any creepy voice call my name in this video. Was there anything like that found? We also didn't see any black shadow or mist."

Harry replied, "Actually there wasn't any EVP capture of your name being called out, but we did capture a voice in the background at the same moment. We'd like you both to listen to that also."

Caroline sat frozen staring at Isabella as tears began to drop down her cheeks. She was an older version of Isabella with the same green eyes and blonde hair. "Isabella, I'm sorry. I'm so sorry for not believing in you and what you've been experiencing. I feel like such a failure as a mother."

"Caroline, you mustn't feel that way. Please know the reaction you had is a normal one. My parents and brothers did the same thing." Marie saw the surprise in Caroline's eyes and continued, "believe me when I tell you, you are not alone in feeling and reacting the way you did. It's only natural not to believe in the un-natural. Don't blame yourself. Isabella doesn't."

"That's right mom. I don't. Marie and the SIPS team are going to help us." Isabella looked at Marie and smiled. "She's going to have me help with investigations and other kids that are struggling with psychic ability."

Marie quickly replied, "That's all still in the works, but we would love to have Isabella's help with our parapsychologist. You remember the woman I mentioned to you the other day, Cheryl Alexander?"

"Yes, I do remember. All of this is just so over-whelming. I still don't understand what happened to my Adam. Why did he see the ball of light and fall into a trance? How could he have seen himself?"

Tim replied, "That's something we haven't quite figured out yet, but we will."

"That's right. We work as a team. You'll soon learn that about us. We're all in this together. We want to learn and understand why paranormal things happen." Mimi grabbed a box of tissues and handed them to Caroline.

"Thank you all so much. I'm not sure I could do any of this alone."

"If it's okay with you, we'd like to have you listen to the EVP that we recorded at the same time the ball of light appeared." Marie handed the earphones to Caroline first and said, "In case you're wondering, an EVP stands for electronic voice phenomenon. It's sometimes not heard with our own ears but captured on our recording devices. They're usually a brief or short word. You'll need to pay close attention, so I want you to watch the clock at the bottom of the screen. When you see it reach two thirty-two point sixteen, you should hear something immediately afterward."

After listening at the appropriate time, Caroline's eyes widened, and she slid the earphones down around her neck. "I think I heard someone ask for help. Is that correct?"

"Yes, that is what we heard as well." Marie handed another pair of earphones to Isabella. "After you're finished you can let Adam listen also."

Both Isabella and Adam heard the same captured EVP. Adam sat back in the chair and began to rub his temples as he left out a sigh. "So why did I see myself?"

Marie looked at the team and then at Adam. "It's tough to say, Adam. There are some theories that what you experienced was a doppelganger effect. What that means is someone being able to see either someone they know or themselves, who is still alive, on the other side of the veil."

Gale rolled her eyes and said, "Marie, Adam looks confused. What she means Adam is that someone on the other side of the veil is someone who is supposed to be dead. A ghost if you will."

"So, I saw myself dead?" Adam's lower lip began to twitch.

Harry replied, "Not really, although the theory is that if you were to see yourself in spirit form, danger or death is forthcoming."

"Harry, we don't know if any of that is true." Mimi stood up and wagged her finger. "That's old folklore and never been proven. Adam, don't worry, you'll be fine. I am a very open-minded person, and I think the doppelganger study is ridiculous."

Caroline moved closer to Adam and put her arm around his shoulders. "I think this is a little much for us to take in. We are very grateful for your investigation and helping us out, and we'd be glad to be a part of helping other children with psychic abilities. But I think we've had enough for one day."

"Yes, of course, I'm very sorry. We tend to get carried away with things. We sometimes forget that not everyone is up-to-speed with the paranormal." Marie glared at Harry and then removed a flash drive from the main computer. "Here, this is a recording for you of our analysis of the investigation. If you have any further questions, and of course, if you experience anything else, please don't hesitate to call us anytime, day or night. We want to be here for you, okay? Remember that you all have control over your home. You just need to simply tell the spirits to leave or cross over into the light. It may sound silly talking to nothing, but it does help."

Isabella stood up and wrapped her arms around Marie. "Thank you. This has been so cool. Can I go on another investigation with you all?"

"That would be up to your mother, Isabella. We won't do anything unless she gives us the go ahead."

Caroline stood up and placed her hands on Isabella's shoulders and said, "Yes, I think I'd like to talk a little more about this with Cheryl Alexander. I still need some time to gather everything I've learned today and maybe speak with a professional if that's okay with everyone?"

"Of course, we absolutely agree. You have Cheryl's card. She's expecting you to call." Marie held out her hand to Caroline. "Don't forget that we're all here for you and your family. This is what we do. We want to help you as much as we can."

The Swanson's left and the team began to close down the computers and pack up the equipment. Marie felt it was time to ask for help from her spirit guides to learn more about these murders and why Isabella is involved. She especially needed guidance from Myra. Is it true Adam saw himself on the other side? Is he in danger? Whatever the answers were, she knew none of it would be going away anytime soon.

CORY IMPATIENTLY WAITED for Sally to arrive at the morgue. The tone of her voice during their conversation left him very curious as to what she had found during the autopsy of the severed head. He looked at the oversized numbers of the clock at the end of the hall and leaned back against the white subway tile wall. She was ten minutes late, and he was anxious to get home to his bride.

He heard the soft shuffling of echoed footsteps and spotted Sally walking toward him dressed in scrubs and shoe covers. She wore a face shield, which was flipped on top of her head revealing a surgical mask covering her nose and chin.

Cory nodded and said, "Hello, you look like you've been knee deep in autopsy mode."

Sally nodded and handed him a surgical mask. "Here, you're going to need this. You're never going to believe what I found."

Cory followed Sally into the stark autopsy room displaying the usual gunmetal gray operating tables. The bright fluorescent lights always bothered his eyes as he squinted against the glare. Even though he'd been doing this for years, he still wasn't used to the smell of chemicals.

Sally removed the sheet revealing the beheaded remains and pulled the protective shield down over her face. "I was able to confirm, as I stated earlier, that this head matches the body found yesterday through the dental records. It has the normal decomposition for sitting in a dumpster in the heat, but the interesting fact is that he didn't die from being decapitated."

Cory's eyebrows went up as he spoke through his mask. "It wasn't? Then what killed him?"

"I didn't want to reveal this until you got here." Sally grabbed the long-toothed forceps and entered the mouth and carefully pulled out a crumpled hundred-dollar bill and placed it on the tray. "This isn't all."

Cory watched her enter the mouth again and saw her pull out a shiny hard-shelled insect and asked, "What the hell is that? Is that a bug?"

"To be exact, it's a beetle, of what type, I'm not sure." She placed it on the tray beside the bill and flipped the face shield, once again, on top of her head. "Now, this hundred is counterfeit. You can already see the acids in the mouth began to erode the lettering here on the corner."

"That coincides with his occupation. So, you're saying this is what killed him? Someone shoved these down his throat and asphyxiated him?"

"Yes, it is, but you need to take a closer look at this beetle." Sally picked up the insect with the forceps and pulled the overhead light down for a better look.

"Can you make out the transparent portions of its body?"

Cory lowered his head and squinted at the golden metallic shelled bug. "Yeah, but why is it down this guy's throat?"

"I have no idea, but someone had a purpose for putting it there."

Cory leaned back up and rubbed his eyes. "Maybe it has some significance in the entomology community?"

"I think the real question is...where did it come from? We have a staffer here that has an odd interest in entomology, and he believes this beetle isn't found here in the United States. He thought this was a mint leaf beetle found in the south of Wales." Sally set the beetle back down on the tray and removed her surgical mask.

"Wherever it came from, and whoever did this, they were making a statement. He must have pissed someone off bad enough to be choked this way. Not to mention chopping off his head." Cory handed the surgical mask back to Sally and walked toward the door. "Thanks again, and I'll look forward to sharing these findings after I get your report. When do you think you'll have it finished?"

"I think I can have it ready for you first thing tomorrow morning."

"Thanks, I appreciate it." Cory nodded his head and walked through the big steel doors. As he approached his car, he said to himself, "To coin an old phrase, this case just became curiouser and curiouser.

. . .

MARIE and the SIPS team gathered around the fire pit in Myra's backyard to discuss the future plans to help children and their parents learn to grasp all the facets involved in having children with psychic abilities and the paranormal. They asked Isabella to be a part of the meeting so she would be able to add her thoughts from a personal aspect.

Tim stirred the logs with a poker and asked, "So where do we begin? Do we need to take official minutes or something?"

Gale rolled her eyes and took a sip of wine. "Seriously, where do you think we are, in a board meeting?"

"That may not be a bad idea. I think it's helpful to have something to go back to as a reference. You never know what great ideas we'll come up with." Marie held up her glass to Tim and toasted him in the air. "Good idea Tim."

"Okay, since it was *Tim's* idea, he can take the minutes." Gale scrunched up her nose and stuck out her tongue.

"I need a pen and paper."

"Are you that helpless?" Gale got up from her chair and walked toward the house. "I'll go see if anything is lying around."

Isabella chuckled and said, "Marie, how did all of you get together? I mean, I remember all of the hangings that took place here a few years ago and how you were hung. But weren't you doing investigations before that?"

Marie replied, "Yes we were, but we had just recently organized the group shortly before all of that. It was a thrill to be able to help solve that case."

"Then that led to you, Gale, Tim and Cory being

invited to do an investigation in New Orleans." Mimi sadly looked at everyone and rubbed Bailey's ears. "That's when all the trouble began."

"What trouble?" Isabella pulled out the pie iron and plopped a gooey s'more onto her plate.

"Without going into too much detail, and for your safety, we encountered a demon while we were in New Orleans. We, or let me rephrase, *I* was pulled into a case involving the occult, which dated back quite a few years ago. I was being sought out by a spirit that had been murdered by this occult." Marie made a deep sigh and continued, "We were able to help with the case, but it almost cost us Gale, and it eventually *did* cost us Myra."

"I thought Myra had a heart attack in DC?"

Gale handed the pen and paper to Tim and said, "She did, but the demon we encountered in New Orleans followed us back here, and finally possessed Myra when we were in Washington."

Harry cuffed his shirtsleeves up to his elbows and then inclined back in the wicker chair. "Isabella, as a demonologist I must warn you to be very careful as you begin this process of learning and growing with your psychic ability. You must take it slow and always listen to Marie and Cheryl's guidance. Most spirits, entities, and the like that you will encounter are good energy, but there is also the potential to get involved with a negative spirit or even a demon. Both good and evil exist."

Jim added, "That's true and even though it sounds like fun to do a paranormal investigation. We do take it seriously and always protect ourselves. We'll help teach you to do the same."

Isabella finished the last bite of her s'more and

said, "Thank you, I feel very comfortable with all of you. You've helped my family and me so much. What was the investigation you had in DC, and how did Myra get possessed there?"

"It was just a matter of time until either Myra or I would come face to face with the demon." Marie finished her beer and placed the bottle on the wicker end table. "By the way, we refuse to state the name of the demon. It's gone for good and speaking its name gives it power, so always remember that."

Tim tapped the pen on the notebook and said, "A woman contacted us in DC to investigate her condo. As it turned out, she really wanted us to help find her missing daughter."

"Oh, that's right. I read that article in The Island Eye News. You guys are famous. You helped bring down the mafia and saved that girl. Cool."

Marie laughed and said, "Well, enough about all of that. We need to get our thoughts together on organizing this...actually, what are we going to call this? Is it a scholarship fund?"

Gale shook her head and said, "I don't think it's an actual scholarship. I mean, it will help kids to learn about their abilities, but it's not like we're giving them money to go to college."

"I agree, and I think we need to figure out how to find these kids. Do we take out an ad?" Mimi ignored the cookies on the tray and grabbed a handful of grapes.

"Wow, this is more involved than I thought." Jim jammed a fistful of peanuts into his mouth and guzzled down the remains of his water.

"Using social media may not be a bad idea. We can also set up a website or blog and begin marketing it through the newspaper and television. It'll take some time." Marie looked at Isabella. "Maybe you can add some of your early personal experiences to the site. I think your viewpoint and outlook would put other children at ease."

"I'd love to help with that. There's a chance there are other kids that live close to us." Isabella grabbed a napkin and wiped the melted marshmallow off her chin.

Harry said, "I'd like to weigh in also."

"Yes, and Cheryl will need to add some clinical aspects too." Marie sat back in the chair and closed her eyes. "Everyone, Myra is here with us. She just told me that she is on board with this idea. She's very pleased."

Isabella's eyes grew wide. "I can feel her. She has such a calm presence."

Gale smiled and winked into the darkness. "That's Myra. She can calm anyone. I think it's great that you're able to communicate with her too."

Mimi pointed to Bailey's tail. "Look, even Bailey can see her."

"Right, let's try to get the details down on what we need on the website and get the information out as soon as possible. Once we begin to get responses, we can organize how to bring them all here. I'll also give Cheryl a call so we can collaborate with her." Marie looked at Tim. "Did you get all of this down?"

"I did, and I'll contact Trevor Mitchell. He's an intern over at the fire station. He's a guru when it comes to designing websites. He redesigned ours."

"Great, it looks as though we've got a lot to get us started. I think it'll all come together. Thanks, every-one, I think we can call it a night. We made great progress." Marie telepathically thanked Myra and her spirit guides. "I'm ready to head home. Cory and I have missed each other coming and going with our schedules. Plus, I believe he has more information on that head they found, so I'm anxious to hear about that."

"Yeah, and let's not forget you're ready to..." Gale caught herself and looked over at Isabella and said, "Fill him in on what we discussed here tonight."

Isabella shook her head and laughed. "I know what you were going to say."

Harry shot up out of his chair. "On that note, I'm ready to head out."

The group laughed, and together they cleared the drinks and food. Tim snuffed out the fire while Jim and Mimi removed the outdoor cushions and placed them in the house. Marie waited until everyone had left and locked the doors and then hooked Bailey's leash to his harness.

As she strolled back to her house, she couldn't help but wonder how things would unfold. She could sense there was much chaos on the other side, which proved difficult for her to stay focused. As well as the chaos taking place on the island.

She chose to clear her mind and think about what Gale alluded to earlier. She was ready to continue where she left off on her wedding night with her husband. That thought had her smiling from ear to ear.

SIX

His body quivered in the night air, but not from a chill, as he stooped in fear and begged for mercy. He never meant to leave the beetle and hundred-dollar bill in Skerrett's throat, but the head was so slimy, and his eyes bugged out after *he* chopped it off. He knew what he'd been told. Didn't it mean anything that he did everything he was asked? He dug all of the holes that he was told to dig. He helped make the counterfeit money and never told anyone what he was doing. He wasn't a snitch. He gave his word, wasn't that good enough?

As the moon disappeared behind the clouds, he lost sight of the reflection from the sword. He tried to move his head off the rock, but the restraints were too tight. He begged again for his life when he heard the quick slice through the air, felt the sharp pain in his neck, and then darkness.

Marie finished her last lap and grabbed the edge of her indoor pool. She began her post-swim stretches and then climbed out and began to dry off. Swimming in the ocean was her original plan, but after listening to the surf report, she decided against it. She was a great swimmer, but it wasn't worth fighting the undercurrent.

She wrapped a towel around her head, slipped into her cotton robe and tiptoed into the kitchen only to find her sexy husband shirtless and frying eggs. She longingly watched his back and shoulder muscles flex as he effortlessly stirred the spatula in the pan. Cory's shorts sat at his hips instantly recreating their long session in bed just a few hours ago as her body immediately reacted to the image playing in her head.

"Wow, now a girl could get used to waking up to this." Marie plopped down into the chair and snagged a piece of sausage off the plate.

Cory turned and gave her a wink. "After a night like we just had, you could get me to do just about anything."

"You're making me blush." Marie looked at the table setting, which consisted of a bowl of fruit, a pitcher of orange juice, sausage, freshly brewed coffee, and a stack of wheat toast. "I didn't realize I had all of this food in the house. I never made it to the grocery store."

"Not a problem, I picked some things up on my way home from the morgue yesterday."

Marie poured a cup of coffee and stirred in some half and half. "Speaking of which, fill me in on the details of the severed head. Or is it too gross to discuss over breakfast?"

"That's up to you." Cory slid the eggs onto a platter and set them in the middle of the tiny kitchen table. "I've become numb to maggot-infested corpses."

Marie scrunched up her face and returned the

strawberry to her plate. "Well, maybe leave out the maggot part."

Cory sat down and began spooning eggs onto Marie's dish and the remaining eggs onto his and said, "Basically Sally stated the head was a definite match to the body. We pretty much figured that, but what we weren't prepared for was a counterfeit hundred-dollar bill and a golden metallic beetle down in his esophagus."

Marie dropped her fork. "Are you kidding me? What the heck was all of that doing in the guy's throat?"

"I'm pretty sure that was meant to be a statement. I think this guy pissed somebody off and whoever killed him wanted him to suffer. Sally said that's what killed him. He suffocated. Then chopping off his head was an afterthought."

"Real nice. What does any of that mean? You said he was in jail for counterfeiting, so maybe he screwed that up, but not sure where the beetle fits in."

"Yeah, that's what Sally and I said. One of the guys in the morgue has a fascination with entomology and stated the beetle isn't from around here. He thinks it's a mint leaf beetle found in the south of Wales."

"What a strange thing to find, and what a horrible way to die."

Cory finished his coffee and slouched back in his chair. "Yeah, this is going to take some time to investigate. We haven't released any of this yet, so we need to keep this under wraps. Hey, you didn't get to fill me in on your plans for helping kids with psychic abilities."

Marie shifted the towel on her head and set her

fork down. "I'll be sure not to share any of the latest findings with anyone, and we had a great meeting. We were able to get Isabella's insight and ideas, as well as everyone else's. They're all on board, including Myra. I think she's pleased with us using her house as a retreat for families. Cheryl Alexander is on board, so that's huge. We need to figure out how to advertise and begin our search for families who need help."

"That's great. This is a commendable thing you're doing."

"Thanks, it feels right, you know?" Marie flinched at the phone ringing and saw her mom's name. She assumed it was to check up to see if she went to church, and not being in the mood to deal with excuses. She left it to go to voicemail.

Cory asked, "You're not going to answer that?"

"No, it's probably Mom. It's Sunday and I don't feel like explaining why I didn't go to church. I'll let her assume that's where I am since it went to voicemail, and if she doesn't ask, I won't have to tell her a white lie."

Cory chuckled and softly touched her hand. "You lay that guilt on yourself. I really don't think your parents expect you to go to church every Sunday. I gather they made it safely home?"

"Yes, they did, and yes you're probably right about my guilt. I'm still working on that."

"I know, so what's the plan for today?"

"I have a short committee meeting later for Carolina days. We just have some small details to iron out." Marie timidly looked at Cory and then quickly shifted her gaze down to her plate. "They asked if I would do readings like Myra did to help raise money."

"That's interesting. How do you feel about that?"

"I'm not sure. I've never really done an actual reading on anyone. I suppose I could try. I think Myra would approve."

Cory squeezed her hand and quickly turned when his cell phone rang. "Who would be bothering me now? Maybe I should let mine go to voicemail."

"Not sure if that's a good idea for the police chief."

"Yeah, you're right." He tapped his phone to answer and put it on speaker. "Hello, this is Chief Miller."

The voice said, "Chief, it's Tom. Sorry to bother you now, but we got a call from Sergeant McMillan from the Folly Island Police Department. It looks like they found another body that matches the same MO as our headless corpse. He asked if we could meet him at the crime scene."

Cory sighed and said, "Okay, give me a chance to change, and I'll meet you there. Do you have the details of where the body was found?"

"Yeah, at the west end of Ashley Avenue in the county park."

"See you in half an hour." Cory disconnected and looked at Marie. "You ready for a road trip?"

Marie shot out of her chair. "Absolutely, can we bring Bailey? I can walk him while you tend to your duties."

"Sure, but let's get a move on."

They both moved in opposite directions to get ready while Bailey wagged his tail in anticipation of a ride. Marie threw on a hat, shorts and a T-shirt and said a quick prayer of protection. She had a strong feeling they were going to need it.

. . . .

MARIE LOOKED at her watch as she took the stairs two at a time and whispered to herself. "I'm only fifteen minutes late, no big deal." She pushed through the door and caught everyone's stare, including Gale, who wore a glare on her face of *I'm going to kill you; where have you been* look. "Sorry everyone, I went out on a police call with Cory. They found another beheaded body on Folly Island."

Genevieve quietly said, "Oh my, that's terrible. I don't think I can deal with another serial killer on the loose."

"Why didn't you call or text me that you were going over there? I could have spent a little more time enjoying what I was doing with Tim." Gale stopped and looked around the room. "Anyway, who'd they find?"

"They're still running the prints through IAFIS. His head was found about twenty feet away."

"Twenty feet away, how on earth did it end up twenty feet away?" Deidra instinctively placed her hand on her neck and shook her head.

Gale snickered, "It rolled, how else?"

"That's just disgusting." Genevieve fixed the pearls around her neck and frowned at Gale.

Marie glared at Gale and said, "Not sure what's going on, but I have to agree with Genevieve, I'm not in the mood to deal with another serial killer around here."

Gale asked, "Hey, speaking of Folly Island, how did it get tagged with the name of Coffin Island?"

Dirk replied, "In September of sixteen ninety-six, Folly Beach was deeded through a royal grant to William Rivers, marking the beginning of an era of private ownership for Folly beach. During the years before the Civil War, the somewhat secluded Folly Beach was known as *Coffin Land*, a name given to the island because it a was a spot where ships that entered Charleston Harbor often left passengers suffering from the plague or cholera. The ships would return on their way back out to sea to pick up survivors and bury the dead. It's also been said that during this pre-war period it served as a hideout for pirates, who rarely received any attention from Charleston, which left the few adventurous permanent residents and the earliest landowners of Folly Beach rule for themselves."

Cam said, "Oh wow, pirates? I love hearing stories about pirates. Which ones were around here?"

Cal looked at Dirk and said, "Actually, Folly Island didn't get the name Coffin Land or Island because of the deaths and burials. It got its name from its ownership by the Coffin family. They were plantation owners in the Beaufort and Charleston counties."

Dirk raised his eyebrow and slowly smiled at Cal and then shifted his eyes back to Cam. "To answer your question, Cam, Blackbeard was known to have frequented Folly Island. I wouldn't want to argue this point with our famed historian, but I've done quite a bit of research through my teachings that prove different. But that's a discussion at a later time. Shall we get back to our meeting please? I have a very busy day ahead of me."

Deidra replied, "Of course, yes let's get back to the matter at hand. Marie, we have everything just about finalized, but we are waiting on your decision to do the readings."

Marie glanced over at Gale and then at Deidra. "I'd be glad to help raise money giving readings. Just fill me in on the process. I've never actually done readings on anyone, but there's always a first."

"Oh, thank you, Marie. The committee surely appreciates your help." Deidra smiled and placed her pen behind her ear.

Gale winked and said, "Yeah, very cool."

Dirk continued to stare at his planner and asked, "Are you as good as Myra?"

Gale turned around in her chair and nearly knocked over her water bottle. "What kind of a question is that? Of course she's as good as Myra. In fact, I think she's better, how about that?"

"Gale, settle down. It's okay, that's a fair question." Marie turned her attention to Dirk who was now looking right at her. "I'm really not sure if I'm as good as Myra. I'm just me, and I don't try to convince skeptics. But if you like, I can give you a reading some time."

Cam nervously shuffled his papers and looked up at Deidra. "Well, let's not get into a big discussion about Marie's abilities. We don't want to forget how she and the SIPS team helped solve the serial killer case a few years back."

"Yes, I think we should wrap up the meeting. Are we adjourned?" Cal smiled at Marie and looked around the table.

Everyone nodded their heads in agreement and began to gather their belongings. Marie shrugged her shoulders at Gale and motioned her head toward the door. She had more information to share with her from the crime scene and had to refrain from telling the group. They needed some girl time and a few margaritas. What better place to do that than Taco Mamacita?

MARIE ENJOYED the warm breeze coming into town from the ocean as she and Gale enjoyed a plate of Memphis Nachos. Taco Mamacita was in the center of town on Middle Street, directly across from Poe's Tavern. The outdoor seating and the ambiance of the lights strung around the ceiling gave a comfy feeling, even though a fence that looked like it contained cattle surrounded the tables. Marie chose a blueberry margarita while Gale sipped down the last remains of the strawberry flavor.

"I think I need another one." Gale looked at Marie's glass and said, "You're behind girl, why are you farming it?"

"I guess I'm still trying to wrap my head around the fact that I'm going to be doing readings on strangers. I've never done that before." Marie hurriedly finished her margarita and waved her hand at the Kewpie Doll looking waitress.

"Don't worry about it. You'll do fine. You always do." Gale stretched her neck to see the protruding nametag pinned to the tight sweater on the waitress. "Mitzi, is it? We'd like another round of margaritas please."

Marie chuckled at Gale's eye roll. "What's the matter, you feel like she's competition in the boob area?"

"Hell no, she's just not proportioned with her five-foot height and double d's." Gale popped a nacho oozing with cheese and jalapeno peppers into her mouth. "Now, what's really got you rattled?"

"For starters, there are spirits all over the place, but one, in particular, is nagging me to tell that guy over there that he made the right decision to buy a boat."

"Some spirit just told you that?" Gale turned around and spotted a handsome gentleman about thirty years in age looking melancholy at his menu. "He's cute. He looks a little sad."

"Yeah, well I've got to go over there and tell him before I get a serious migraine." Marie nodded at the spirit and then stood next to the gentleman.

"Okay, but if you're not back by the time your margarita is here, I can't say that I'll be able to keep from drinking any."

Marie returned and sat back down and glared at Gale. "You drank some of mine, didn't you?"

"I said I couldn't help myself. I may have to get a blueberry one next." Gale winked and said, "So what'd the guy say?"

"It was his wife trying to communicate with him. She passed away from lymphoma cancer last year. She had a large life insurance policy, and she wanted him to quit feeling guilty that he spent some of the money on a boat."

"Oh wow, did he freak out?"

"A little at first, but after I explained and acknowledged her presence, he was blown away...and thankful."

"See and you wondered how you'd do readings on strangers. Now, what else is on your mind? You looked a bit preoccupied in the meeting. I can't deny I was a little ticked off at professor snooty pants questioning your ability. I don't trust him. Cal whispered to me after the meeting that Dirk is about as friendly as dog shit on your boot. He cracks me up."

"That pretty much describes Dirk. I do appreciate you coming to my defense, but that doesn't bother me anymore. What did have me preoccupied was how they found this latest body. He was found with his hands chained to a huge rock, and then Cory told me earlier the ME found a counterfeit hundred-dollar bill and a beetle shoved down Skerrett's throat."

"Whoa, why would someone shove that down Skerrett's throat and why was this second victim chained to a rock? That sounds like they were both being punished. What the hell is going on around here?"

"I don't know, but it had Cory shook up. Which, by the way, I didn't tell the group so keep those details quiet please?"

"Sure, no problem, I can keep a secret. Don't roll your eyes at me. So does Cory have any other leads?"

"No, and I'm not getting any feel from these murders. I mean, in the past I've had spirits come to me. Nothing seems to be happening. It's like I'm closed off on this."

"Well, don't try to force anything. That usually makes things worse for you." Gale sucked her straw and immediately grabbed the bridge of her nose. "Ouch, brain freeze, man I hate when I do that."

"You're almost finished with your second one. No wonder you got a brain freeze."

"Yeah, part of the hazards of drinking frozen margaritas. So, are you happy with our plans to help kids with psychic abilities? Has anyone answered our ad?"

"I am very excited about doing this, and I need to

check my email account on the blog we created. I haven't had a chance. It's been pretty crazy around here lately." Marie finished her margarita and pushed her glass to the side of the table. "That's it for me. Speaking of crazy, I forgot to tell you that SIPS got another inquiry to do an investigation at The Old Village Post House in Mount Pleasant."

"Oh, wow, seriously? I've heard all kinds of stories about that place."

"Yeah, the new owners, David and Dayna Kingsburg, really don't want that reputation but they can't ignore what's been going on. Dayna said there are sounds of little children playing in the hall, and some of the employees feel uneasy on the third floor. She said it's disturbing the overnight guests."

"I bet it is. Did you set up a time?"

"No, I thought I'd bring it up at tomorrow night's meeting. I don't think anyone will have a problem. I'd like to ask if Isabella would like to go."

"That's a great idea. Of course, we need to bring Bailey."

"Of course, we can't do an investigation without him." Marie watched Mitzi place the check on the table and then quickly snatched it up before Gale had a chance to grab it. "This one is on me. You paid for drinks at Poe's Tavern the other night."

"Hey, I'm not arguing." Gale stood up, grabbed her purse, and slung it over her shoulder. "Come on, let's get out of here. I always feel like mooing when I sit outside in this corral."

Marie laughed and shook her head. "I'm not even going there on the moo comment."

"You'd better not."

Marie followed Gale out toward the street and

took delight in the fact they could walk back to their homes. It was great living so close to town center, plus it was better to walk off the buzz she was feeling than get pulled over, which would look pretty bad being married to the police chief.

SEVEN

MARIE LOVED to watch the SIPS team in meeting mode when they discussed possible investigations. It always amazed her to see this eclectic group come together with each of their talents to help a client.

Isabella sat wide-eyed watching the team pull resources from the Internet on The Old Village Post House. She slowly walked over to Harry and looked over his shoulder. "What exactly are you doing?"

Harry nervously fixed his bow tie and said, "We like to search for any links that tie into place with the investigation so we can rule out any false claims. We prefer to go and pull real records on a home or business as opposed to listening to the legends or stories that people tell. Even though personal claims are important, we like to make sure we have all the facts. We go into every investigation with an open mind, so we don't contaminate anything."

"How can you contaminate it?"

Mimi replied, "We don't want to be pulled in one direction or another from a story or claim. We take it all in and learn as much as we possibly can, but we don't want to be swayed by a certain story or experience that someone else had. We first like to see if we can debunk a claim, but if we're able to record the same experience either on our cameras or voice recorders, then all the better. Does that make sense?"

"Yeah, I think so. You want to be sure to have a clear head so you can be objective."

"Exactly, very good, I think you're going to fit in very well with us Isabella." Marie winked and turned to the group. "Okay everyone, if you've pulled all of your information on The Old Village Post House, I'd like to organize a date and time that works best for everyone to do the investigation."

Gale set her empty glass down on the long conference table and plopped into a chair. Her rich sable hair was held ponytail style by a green silk scarf. "The only information I know about the place is that the food is amazing."

"The rooms are pretty cool too, although I didn't have any experiences when I stayed there." Tim's sleeves pulled at the seams as he moved his arms into a folded position.

Gale's one eyebrow cocked. "When did you ever stay there? It wasn't with me."

Tim quickly replied, "I was in Steve Morelli's wedding a few years ago. It was before you and I met...and I was alone."

Gale smirked and said, "Mhmm."

"Okay, well let's get back to important issues, shall we?" Marie ignored Gale's snarl and continued, "Jim and Mimi have an appointment with Cynthia Brown over at the Mount Pleasant's Historical Society, which will give us more insight into the history of the establishment. Harry, did you find anything regarding legends or folklore?"

Harry removed his cloth medical taped glasses and wiped his lenses with his overused handkerchief and placed them back on his nose. "No, only a site stating it was haunted, but nothing in detail, which is a good thing."

"Great, sounds like we're rolling along with everything. Is there a preferable date and time for anyone to investigate? Dayna stated that it didn't matter to them, they're not going to be able to shut down, so we'll have to consider that when we investigate."

After a bit of a discussion, Marie typed the date and time into the calendar on her smartphone and said, "A week from this Saturday it is. I'll give Dayna a call to confirm. The next thing I'd like to do is go over the equipment with Isabella. Since she's going to be joining us on this investigation, she'll need to be up-to-speed on what we use."

Isabella smiled and said, "Oh that sounds cool, I'd love to learn how to use the laser grid."

"Great, we'll start you out on that. Tim or Jim can teach you. They've used it the most and understand how to explain the way any movement or change in a room can be detected from a disturbance within the laser grid pattern." Marie stood up from her chair and turned toward the sound of a cell phone ringing. "Is that mine or someone else?"

Isabella sheepishly grabbed her phone from her pocket. "It's mine. I'm so sorry."

"Not a problem, the ring sounded close to mine. Go ahead and answer it." Marie watched Isabella's face contort as she quickly walked over and placed her hand on Isabella's shoulder. "Is everything okay?"

Isabella shot up from her chair and grabbed her jacket. "I have to go home now. That was my mom. She just said that Adam is threatening to jump off the roof of our building. She's hysterical. She said he keeps mumbling something about the voices told him he has to jump."

Marie looked at the team and said, "Isabella we'll all come with you. Let me drive you. We'll get there faster. Everyone, it looks like they need our help. Harry, you're going to need to get your counselor game-face on."

Within minutes the team arrived at Isabella's condo. They walked around to the side of the building and saw Caroline looking up at the roof with tears streaming down her face. A small crowd of people was standing with her yelling up to Adam.

Marie walked over to Caroline and asked, "When did this start for Adam hearing these voices and how long has he been on the roof?"

Caroline wiped her face with her arm and sucked in a breath. "I don't know when the voices started, but about ten minutes ago he came running out of his room screaming and holding his hands over his ears. He was asking for Isabella and kept saying he has no head."

Marie calmly took Isabella by the hand and walked in front of the crowd. "Isabella, I want you to calmly call your brother's name and at the same time telepathically call him. Right now, you can see he's staring out into oblivion, so you'll know when you get his attention."

Isabella took in a deep breath and quietly said, "Adam, look at me. Can you please look at me?"

Marie saw Adam snap out of his trance and then look down at Isabella. "Good, Isabella, you have his attention. Now ask him to come down the emergency ladder carefully. He's still fragile, so don't raise your voice or your telepathic vibration."

Adam slowly cocked his head to the side and carefully sat down on the roof and slid over to the ladder. He climbed down, and when his feet hit the ground, he wrapped his arms around Isabella and began to cry. "I kept calling for you, but nothing came out of my mouth."

Isabella squeezed Adam tight as tears slipped down her cheeks. "It's okay Adam. I'm here now. We're all here. Why don't we go inside?"

Harry looked at Marie and said, "You did great, Marie. You guided Isabella to do the exact right thing. I couldn't have done it any better myself."

"Thanks, Harry, it just popped into my head that Isabella was the key to getting him down off the roof." Marie looked at Gale. "I'm going to go in with them, would you mind going back with everyone and clearing up the room? We were pretty much done with our meeting. I need to get to the bottom of this."

"Absolutely, we'll take care of it and lock up. I'll make sure Bailey's all set too."

"Would you also mind giving Cory a call at the station? Let him know I may be a while."

"Will do, and Marie, be careful. You know something is going on that brings Adam into these murders. He wouldn't have mentioned someone not having a head, right?"

"I thought the same thing, and I also think Isabella isn't telling us everything she knows."

Gale nodded her head. "I think it's time you tap into Myra and your guides. The other side needs to step in and help before there's another murder."

"Agreed, I'll catch up with you later." Marie walked around the brick building to Isabella's condo and lightly rapped on the door that held a fluorescent plastic number six.

Caroline opened the door and robotically motioned for Marie to come inside. "I hope you can help them."

Marie graciously smiled and walked over to the couch where Isabella held Adam in her arms and sat down. "How's he doing?"

Without looking up, Isabella said, "He's okay now, but his heart is racing."

"I bet. He's lucky to have you as a sister." Marie leaned forward and looked straight into Isabella's eyes. "I believe that Adam is being sought out by something or someone concerning these murders. But he's not the one they need to talk with, is he?"

Isabella slowly shook her head as tears filled the rim of her eyes. "No, they're using him to get my attention."

"That's right, and I think you need my help to understand that everything is going to be okay and it's safe to speak with them." Marie grabbed Isabella's hand and felt a jolt shoot up her arm. "Isabella, a gentleman is trying to speak to you. He has appeared to you with no head, but you need to calmly see him. Once you let go of that fear, you'll see him as whole. Can you do that for me?"

Isabella slowly nodded her head and then let out a breath. "Oh, there he is, he's not creepy looking anymore."

"That's right, and he has a message for you that he's been trying to tell you. Can you try to calm your mind and clear your thoughts? Once you do, you'll be able to channel yourself to his vibration."

Isabella closed her eyes and took in a deep breath. "He says he didn't mean to do it and that he's sorry. He only did what he was told. I can't hear him plainly anymore. He's scared. He's gone now."

"That's okay. You were fantastic. You're beginning to understand how to handle your ability. How does that make you feel?"

"A little freaked out but excited at the same time."

Marie chuckled and said, "That's about right. Now, what we need to do is have you describe him. Without thinking, I want you to give me what you can remember about how he looked, and I'll put it into my phone. Don't leave out any details."

Isabella said, "He had dark brown hair and was tall, like Adam. He was wearing a T-shirt and jeans. I can't make out his eyes. They were hollow. Wow, that's strange."

"What's strange?"

"This may not make any sense, but his hands were chained together."

Marie's eyes grew large as she stopped typing into her phone. "Isabella, that isn't strange at all. You see, what nobody knows and what the police have not said is that this latest victim's body was found chained to a rock. It's pretty obvious you just communicated with the second murder victim."

MARIE LAY on her side and leaned on her elbow as she watched Cory's chest rise and fall. It was the greatest feeling to wake up to him every day. It gave her a sense of calm, especially in the middle of chaos. As she slowly moved to get up, she felt his hand softly grab her thigh, and she smiled and said, "I hope I didn't wake you."

"You did, but that's okay, I love waking up to you." Cory propped a pillow under his head and pulled Marie close to his side. "Where did you think you were going?"

"I thought I'd get the coffee started. I forgot to set the timer last night when I got home. I was too exhausted. I wanted to share with you what happened, but you were sawing logs."

"Gale told me about Adam and that you were helping him and Isabella. She said you suspected Isabella knew a little more than what she let on. She also said you have a date for your investigation at the Old Village Post House."

Marie ran her fingers through his chest hairs. "Adam was just a conduit for the time being until Isabella finally accepted that she was being contacted by a spirit. They were using Adam to get her attention. It finally worked. Adam on the roof threatening to jump put it all into perspective, and yes, we're going to do the investigation next Saturday. Are you going to be able to come?"

"I don't think so. This case has everyone on their toes and on-call twenty-four seven."

"I thought that might be the deal, that's okay, we'll keep you posted, but I didn't tell you the most interesting piece of information about Isabella."

"What's that?"

"That she's being sought out by the latest murder victim."

Cory sat straight up and asked, "She saw this guy, and you didn't?"

"I know right, that's what blew my mind, but they'll reach out to anyone who has this ability. Spirits aren't picky and they won't let up until they're heard."

"What did you find out?"

Marie sat up and shifted against the headboard. "She described the man as being tall like her brother Adam, so I guess five foot nine with brown hair."

"That describes a lot of people."

"Yeah, well he had no head at first, but the spot-on detail was that his hands were chained together."

Cory turned and said, "You're kidding me? No, I know that answer. Nobody knew that but those of us on the scene and you. Okay, it looks like we'll be working with you and Isabella on this case because his prints came up with a match."

"And?"

"His name was James Lawson, and he was in the same prison as Skerrett. Don't know if they knew each other, but I think we can be pretty sure that they did. He wasn't in for counterfeiting like Skerrett, but he had a long list of priors. What landed him in jail was rape and burglary."

"That's disgusting."

"Yeah, it is. We need to find what ties these two together. We'll be doing some more interviews. Maybe we can both talk a little more with Isabella if you think she's up to it. How was Adam when you left?"

"He fell straight to sleep. I think he'll be okay now that Isabella understands she's got to be open to Lawson trying to communicate with her. I know she'd be more than happy to help out on the case. She's got a better handle on her ability than I ever did at that age." Marie sat at the edge of the bed.

"Again, I ask, where do you think you're going?" Cory ran his hand up and down Marie's back.

"As I said earlier, I thought I'd get the coffee on. I also need to get ready to set up for tomorrow. June twenty-eight is the anniversary of the Battle of Sullivan's Island...Carolina Days."

"I don't think so." Cory leaned over and began to kiss Marie's shoulder.

"Oh, I see, well I suppose the coffee can wait."

"You're damn right the coffee can wait."

Marie giggled and fell back against Cory's chest and let him take control of the situation, at least that's what she let him believe.

ISABELLA JUMPED out of bed and stared at the headless spirit. She remembered Marie's words to remain calm and state her intention of how she wished to be approached. She telepathically asked for him to appear as he was before he lost his head. Within a few seconds, he looked normal, at least as normal as a dead person could look.

His mouth was moving in a rapid motion, and she had to raise her vibration to pick up on his words. Everything was muddled and strange so she grabbed a pen and piece of paper and tried to write down as much as she could. She felt herself fall into a trance as her hand scribbled the information she heard onto the paper.

When the spirit had disappeared, Isabella looked down at the page and saw what she had written. It made absolutely no sense, but as she looked at what she just wrote, she needed to talk with Marie and the SIPS team to see if they could decipher this gibberish.

53000305))6*;4826)o.)40);806*;480860))85;;]8*;:o*8o8
(88)5*o;46(;88*96*?;8)*o(;485;5*o2:*o(;4956*2(5*__4)£

EIGHT

It was great to see the community of Sullivan's Island come together to celebrate the annual commemoration of the Battle of Sullivan's Island on June twenty-eight, seventeen seventy-six. The fight took place at what is now Fort Moultrie and many historians, including Cal, believed it was the first significant American victory over the British during the revolution.

Everything was in full swing at the fort, which included musket and artillery demonstrations, period medical programs, portrayal by members of the Second South Carolina regiment of how a Revolutionary War soldier's life would have been during that time, and then an evening concert given by the Two Hundred Forty Sixth Army Band.

There were white canvas camp tents lined up in rows depicting how the soldiers would have lived in sweltering temperatures. Living historians shared what types of food were eaten during that time, as well as marching in formation to give an artillery demonstration. The entire town buzzed with sounds of musket fire and cannons, smells of campfire cooking, and visions of children and adults learning about their history.

Outside of the fort, the town celebrated in different ways with businesses sharing their wares in style and restaurants boasting their fantastic food. Marie wore a mint green sleeveless maxi dress with ivory sandals and sat outside of Elyssa Morgan's business and did what she did best, people watch. It was one of her favorite things to do, especially now that spirit was part of the scene. Elyssa was a massage therapist and a dear friend to Myra. She agreed to allow Marie to continue the psychic readings in the back room of her establishment.

Marie adjusted the sign that read, *fifteen-minute psychic reading*, and spotted Gale sashaying down the sidewalk in a pair of salmon Capris and a navy peplum top. "Hello there, girlfriend, how are you?"

Gale slid her sunglasses down her nose and looked at the sign. "This thing needs repainted. It hasn't changed since Myra did these readings."

"I was thinking the same thing. Depending on how well these readings go, maybe I'll give it a makeover."

"Gee, for someone so confident in certain things, you sure are pessimistic about your ability to do the readings today, how come?"

Marie sighed and said, "Oh, I don't know. You're right. I need to work on that. I know I have the ability, a classic example is I can see spirit walking around town following their loved ones."

Gale stomped up the steps in her wedged platform sandals and sat next to Marie. "Now that *is* classic. Who are you seeing? Can you hear what they're saying? Fill me in on all the gossip."

Marie chuckled and rolled her eyes. "I don't hear any gossip. It's a bit garbled. I need to focus on clearing my thoughts for these readings, so I'm trying to tune them out. But it still fascinates me sometimes."

"Such as..."

"Okay, do you remember Leslie Shaffer? She used to teach at the elementary school in Mount Pleasant." Marie continued after Gale's nodded response. "Her mother was following her and nattering in her ear about the money she gave to her husband for his business. Apparently, it's not doing so well."

"Now see, that's what I'm talking about, juicy gossip. What else did you hear?"

Marie shifted on the deck step and rested her shoulder against the railing. "That was all I could hear. My head is buzzing enough as it is."

Gale removed her sunglasses and placed them in her Coach bag and pointed to the street. "Is that Isabella coming this way? She looks upset."

"I think it is. She has a piece of paper in her hand." Marie watched Isabella tug at her shirt and flip her hair back behind her shoulders as she approached where they were seated. "Hello Isabella, what brings you by today? Is everything okay?"

Isabella gave a faint smile, shrugged, and stopped right at the foot of the deck stairs. "I'm not sure how I am. I had that headless goof of a spirit visit me last night. It freaked me out because he didn't have a head at first, so I remembered how you explained to me about asking them to appear *normal*. Then I saw him with a head, but I couldn't understand what he was saying. And then I began to focus on his words, and I suddenly found myself grabbing a pen and paper and writing down this mumbo jumbo."

Marie took the paper Isabella handed her and asked, "What the heck is all of this? It looks like a bunch of numbers and symbols."

Gale reached over and grabbed the paper and squinted at the message. "Okay, now this *is* really strange. What does it mean?"

"I have no idea. I didn't even know I was writing it. I felt woozy and sort of in a trance, and the next thing I knew, this was written down. Obviously, I wrote it." Isabella slumped down on a step and let out a big sigh.

"Okay, before we try and rack our brains to understand what this means, we'll need to run this by the team. I think Harry may be able to help us out. Maybe it's something from the bible. Isabella, if you don't have anything to do today, you're more than welcome to stick around here with me. This would be a great learning experience for you. It'd give you some exposure to learn to channel. You may even see things that I don't."

Isabella stood straight up and nearly knocked Gale over. "You'd let me help you do readings on people?"

"Absolutely, I think I'd enjoy the company."

Gale slid her purse over her shoulder and stepped down onto the sidewalk. "On that note, I'm off. I'm supposed to help with the information booth at the fort. I need to relieve Deidra. Why did I let you talk me into being on this committee? I could be at home or over at Tim's playing."

"Let's keep this conversation PG rated, shall we?"

Marie winked and shooed Gale away with her hand. "This is great character building for you to volunteer your time."

"That's what you wanted to say to me? I need character building?" Gale turned and sauntered toward the street and said, "See you, ladies, later."

"I'll fill you in on how everything goes. Let's get together later with the guys for some drinks." Marie smiled at Gale's thumbs-up reply.

Isabella giggled and said, "She looks like Frankenstein with a bad hip walking in those shoes."

Gale yelled back to them as she turned the corner. "I heard that."

TIM LOOKED TANNED and relaxed in his blue khaki shorts and a teal polo shirt as he stared at the sheet of paper and said, "This just looks familiar to me somehow."

"Where have you seen it before?" Marie slowly sipped her wine and sat down in the sky-blue Adirondack chair in Gale's backyard facing the ocean. The sound of the waves always brought her peace.

"I'm not sure. I've read many books over my lifetime, I can't remember. But I know I've seen this from something I've read."

Gale brought out a tray of bruschetta with tomato and basil. "Tim, what haven't you read? By the way Marie, I forgot to tell you I love that maxi dress. The color is great on you."

"Thank you and this white wine from the Arrigoni wine family hit the spot. Maybe Cory will have an idea what this means when he gets here, which should be soon. He had some interviews today to learn more about the second victim. They're not making any headway." Marie grabbed a baguette flooded with tomatoes and carefully took a bite.

Tim asked, "You ladies didn't say anything about your day. Marie, how'd the readings go and Gale, how'd you do at the information booth?"

"I was bored out of my head at the information booth. Nobody came by to ask any questions. I'm not even sure why you need a booth." Gale poured a glass of merlot and sat on a cushioned bench beside the wooden picnic table. "The only information people are interested in is about these murders. Everyone's worried about another killing spree."

"First of all, it *is* important for an information booth, and secondly, I agree about everyone being worried. That's pretty much the topic of conversation before and after the readings I gave, which went well." Marie slipped a corner of bread to Bailey. "Isabella did a great job also. She's got a decent handle on her ability. I was pleasantly impressed."

Tim grabbed a handful of pretzels, popped them into his mouth, then chugged down the rest of his beer. He finished chewing and said, "That's great to hear. I think she's going to be a real asset on our investigations, as well as helping with other kids."

"I agree." Marie saw Cory come through the sliding door and waved. "Hello there, stranger, glad you could join us."

Cory smiled and immediately removed his uniform tie and unbuttoned the top two shirt buttons. "I am seriously ready for a beer. I didn't get to really enjoy my burger from Poe's, too much paperwork."

"Marie said you were doing interviews. How did all of that go, any leads?" Gale opened a beer and handed it to Cory.

Cory took a gulp, kissed Marie on the forehead, and sat down on the bench next to Gale. "Thank you, this is just what I needed, and yes the interviews were long and of no help. We learned the second victim is John Lawson, so we interviewed guys who had served time with him and Skerrett, but they're not giving us much to go on. They're hiding something, but we'll squeeze them enough to give us what we need."

"You usually do." Marie smiled and said, "We were filling each other in on our day. Gale was bored, as usual, at the information booth. I did pretty well with my readings. I think I raised a fair amount of money for the committee. But the biggest news of all was what Isabella brought to Gale and me earlier today."

Cory grabbed the paper Marie handed him and read what was written and then set it on the table. "Okay, I give, what does it mean? What has it got to do with Isabella?"

"That's what we're trying to figure out. Tim seems to think he's seen it somewhere before." Marie picked up the paper again and shook her head. "Isabella had another visit from the headless Lawson. She said he was trying to talk to her and before she knew it, she was grabbing a pen and paper and wrote this down. She doesn't even remember doing it."

"Isn't that what they call automatic writing?" Gale dipped a carrot in some sour cream and ranch dressing and licked the excess from her lips.

"Yes, it is. We discussed that between readings

today. I've never been able to do that, but I'd like to help her home in on that ability. When I handled the paper, I thought I'd get a read on it using psychometry, but I could only pick up on things about Isabella. I'm really in the dark on this one."

Cory asked, "Is she doing any better with seeing headless Lawson? I know you said it freaked her out."

"She is, and she's doing very well with controlling her ability. She's so much more in-tune than I was at her age."

Tim abruptly sat up and nearly knocked over his plate of bruschetta. "*The Gold Bug*, that's where I remember seeing those symbols, I think it's from Edgar Allen Poe's, *The Gold Bug*."

"Are you sure? How on earth can you remember something like that?" Gale got up from the bench and set her glass on the picnic table. "There's one way to find out, I've got a copy of that book in my shop. I can't remember what edition it is, but its leather bound and pretty cool looking. Let me go get it, and we can compare it to what Isabella wrote."

Marie asked, "What on earth would the connection be to that story? I'm not even sure if I remember it all, other than it being about Captain Kidd hiding treasure here on the island."

"That's about the gist of it, but these symbols were supposed to be a hidden code to the location of the treasure, like a cryptogram." Tim grabbed another handful of pretzels and popped three at a time into his mouth.

"I must say, I'm amazed at how much you retain from the things you read." Cory shook his head.

"Don't ask him to remember a loaf of bread or a

quart of milk." Gale walked back over to the table and placed a burgundy leather-bound book with gold embossed letters that read *The Gold Bug*. "Here it is. I'll leaf through and see if we can find the symbols. I think I read this book in high school."

"We were just discussing the storyline. I'm not quite sure what it has to do with the murders, but we can be sure it'll tie in with my vision or this case." Marie watched Gale turn the fragile pages of the book and quickly pointed and said, "There, there it is, as plain as day. Wow, Tim, you are amazing. Here's the paper that Isabella wrote, does it match?"

Gale held the paper on the opposite page and compared the written text. "It's not identical, but it's pretty damn close. A few of these symbols are different, but most of them look the same. How in the world was she able to write this down? I have to agree with you, Marie. There's a connection here."

"I think we need to share this with Isabella and the team, but it'll have to wait until our investigation. Maybe we can chat in between investigating." Marie continued to stare at the symbols.

Tim said, "You do realize the story explains how there were skeletons found buried beside the treasure, and that Captain Kidd had to have been the murderer."

"Why did he commit the murders?" Gale continued to search through the book and began to read a few of the pages.

"It was rumored the men murdered helped Kidd dig the trench to hide the treasure, but he didn't want them to reveal the location. So, he buried them with the treasure."

Cory asked, "Yes, but this was all pure fiction,

right? Poe was an alcoholic and a drug addict. Nobody really believes the story. Do they?"

"Actually, Poe wasn't either of those things. There's been evidence that was a myth and Poe's enemies told those slanderous lies to defame him. Quite a few myths are flying around out there about Poe." Tim smiled and shrugged his shoulders. "Sorry, I said I read a lot."

Gale did an eye roll and said, "Yes, so we've learned. I had no idea I was dating such a literary hunk."

"Again, the question we aren't able to answer is why and what do these symbols have to do with our headless Lawson. Plus, does any of it tie in with Marie's original vision of the skeletons she saw on a beach?" Cory looked at Marie and said, "Have you had any visions or gotten any type of a read from Myra?"

"No, I haven't, and that's pretty frustrating to me. I think I'll need to work a little more with Isabella." Marie sat back down on the chair and finished the last drop of her wine. "My curiosity gets the better of me trying to figure out what a counterfeiter and a rapist have to do with any of this. Not to mention that counterfeit hundred-dollar bill and beetle they found in Skerrett's throat, and Isabella seeing Lawson's spirit with chains on his wrists."

Tim asked, "A counterfeit hundred and a beetle, and what chains on whose wrist? I didn't hear anything about that."

Marie awkwardly looked at Cory and said, "Sorry, I wasn't supposed to say anything. That hasn't been released to the public yet."

Gale said, "And you thought I couldn't keep a secret."

Cory replied, "That's okay, I can trust Tim. This second victim, Lawson, was found with his wrists chained together, and Isabella described the spirit she sees the same way. When Dr. Brasher did the autopsy on Skerrett's head, she found a counterfeit hundred and beetle down his esophagus. There's no doubt this was done to make a statement, and without being able to connect these two victims we're still not any further in the case, which has my butt in a sling. The other odd thing is one of the guys in the morgue thinks the beetle is a mint leaf beetle, which isn't indigenous to this area."

Tim asked, "Where can it normally be found?"

"He said in the south of Wales."

Gale began to gather the empty glasses and bowls and placed them on the tray. "I'm not sure I believe what any of this has to do with this story. Cory's right, it *is* a fictional story, and there's been no treasure ever found on Sullivan's Island."

"That's true, but there is some relevance, this writing from Isabella and now the beetle, even though the symbolism of the beetle in the story represents a skull." Marie walked over and sat down next to Cory. "It looks like we're being pulled in, yet again, to another case. I hope we can shed some light and give you some leads from the spiritual side, because there isn't a lot of help here in the natural. Maybe we all need to re-read *The Gold Bug* and try to decode this message. Who knows, there may be some clues that could help us."

. . .

STARING at the skull helped him to relax. The glow from the fire filtered through the eye socket casting an eerie shadow against the wall. Nobody understood him. Nobody gave him the respect he deserved. He took a sip of scotch and let it linger on his tongue before allowing it to drift down the back of his throat. Soon they'll see. Soon they'll understand.

NINE

THE OLD VILLAGE Post House sat at the corner of Venning and Pitt Street in the historic fishing town of Mount Pleasant, SC. Tucked in the neighborhood with its white wood siding and black shutters, it boasted the warm feeling of history and comfort. The tall windows that lined the first floor were fitted with plantation shutters while the cast iron planters on the front sidewalk held a host of vibrant colored flowers. If the business sign hadn't been adorned over the door, one would think it was just another quaint home found in town.

The wide double door entry welcomed you into a large open dining room with aged yellow pined planked floors that creaked under your feet. The ceiling, with its exposed beams, and the walls had the original wainscoting. The chandeliers were stemmed in copper with wicker globed lights that cast a warm glow over the room, and the square tables were covered in white linen, which gave a pleasing contrast to the golden-hued paisley upholstered tall back dining chairs.

The sun hung just above the horizon as the SIPS

team parked in front and began unloading their equipment while Bailey sniffed and explored for a good spot to relieve himself. The warm summer breeze hit the back of Marie's neck as she grabbed the file from the backseat and proceeded to the dining area and spotted a slender woman in her fifties with short-cropped brunette hair. Marie smiled as the woman approached, met her extended hand, and said, "I'm Marie Bartek, I mean Miller, co-founder of SIPS. You must be Dayna Kingsburg."

Dayna's brown eyes danced as she smiled and excitedly shook Marie's hand. "Yes, I am. It's so nice to meet you. We've heard such great things about your group. I hope you can help us out."

Marie squeezed her arm against her side to keep the case file from falling to the floor as she released Dayna's hand. "I hope we can help you too. We're very excited that you asked us here. We'd like to do a walk-through first and note where the hot spots are, and then we'll begin to place our cameras and digital recorders in those areas."

"That sounds great, and we have some snacks and drinks here for your team to boost your energy throughout the evening. I'm sure ghost investigating creates a hunger."

Tim replied, "Absolutely, and thank you for that."

Gale smirked and whispered. "You're just in your glory around food."

Marie ignored Gale and followed Dayna into the side hall and asked, "Is this the hall you spoke of over the phone where children's footsteps have been heard?"

Dayna pointed toward the top of the stairs. "It's actually at the other end by rooms five and six. We

103

had a psychic here a few years back, and she claimed the spirit that lingered here was named Richard. He was German and a bit abusive toward his wife. He owned the store where the pub is now. The psychic helped him to cross over, but we still seem to get reports of activity. It's terrible to have your guests startled during their stay. We haven't had anyone leave in the middle of the night, but it certainly creates a topic of conversation over breakfast."

Marie motioned for Harry to come over as she wrote in her notebook. "Let's be sure to have a camera here angled toward the top of the stairs and another in the hall by rooms five and six."

"Got it, oh and Isabella asked to see you when you were finished." Harry placed an X with painter's tape on the floor marking where the camera would stand.

"Okay, I'll have Gale walk with Dayna to learn where the hot spots are." Marie smiled at Dayna and said, "I need to chat with one of the team members. I'll send Gale over to do the walk-through."

Dayna said, "Oh that's fine. I'm so excited to see if your team will capture anything."

Marie smiled and then walked over to where Isabella sat uncoiling an extension cord. Her hair was tied back in a ponytail, and she wore matching black leggings, a sweater, and combat boots.

Marie asked, "Hey is everything okay?"

"I'm not sure. Are you seeing any spirits walking around?"

Marie chuckled and said, "Yes, it's hard to miss them. You need to ignore them and state your intent and ask them to give you some space. What you and I *can't* do is bring any of those elements into the case. We have to record and document everything we can for the client. Even though we can see and hear spirits, we don't want to contaminate the investigation."

"I understand. It just gets a little overwhelming sometimes."

"Isabella, I need you to be completely honest with me. Your mother permitted you to go on this investigation, but I want to be sure you're okay with it. I need to know you're a hundred percent sure you want to be here. It's completely your call. The second you begin to feel uneasy in any way I need to know. Do you understand?"

Isabella shook her head yes and said, "I'm totally okay with it. Really, I am. As long as you're here, I feel more confident."

"Good, and please know you've got the support from the entire team here for you, okay?"

Isabella stood up, grabbed the extension cord, and draped it over her shoulder. "I know, and thanks. It just got a little weird there for a minute. I need to take this over to Tim. I'm helping him set up the laser grid."

"Tim's a great teacher, be sure to listen and learn. It's a great piece of equipment." Marie walked over to Gale and said, "Hey can you please finish the walk-through with Dayna? I need to stay close to Isabella. She's having a little difficulty dealing with spirit. They're trying to invade her space. I'd like to alleviate any fear she may have."

Gale stuck out her bottom lip in a childish pout and said, "Awe I don't want to do the walk-through. You know I zone-out on the walk-through. I'd rather get the equipment set up."

"Look I don't have time for you and your whining.

Please just go and do as I ask. She's a great lady, and she's our client, okay?"

"Okay, don't get all huffy. I'm going...I'm going." Gale flipped her hair back, immediately stuck out her chest, and sauntered over to Dayna.

Marie shook her head and walked over to Mimi and Jim and offered to help check the batteries in the digital recorders while the team continued to set up the equipment. They chose to have headquarters outside in the utility van since there were claims reported throughout the entire building.

Marie did a last-minute check on the main computer of all the camera angles. She grabbed the two-way radio and said, "Okay team, the cameras look great. Why don't we have Jim and Harry head on up to the third floor, while Mimi and Tim take Bailey in the patio area? Gale, Isabella and I will stay at command central."

The radio cracked, and Jim's voice came through and said, "Copy, heading up to the third floor now."

Tim replied, "That's a copy."

Isabella sat next to Marie and stared at the screen of five separate camera shots located throughout the inn. "What exactly do we do here in the van? Isn't it kind of boring?"

Gale said, "Yeah, it can get a little boring, depends on who you're with in the van."

"Ignore her, and although it may seem boring, it's very important we watch the monitors. There are times we catch things here on a screen that a team member doesn't see while investigating. If that happens, we radio them what took place, and then we mark it here in the notebook."

"There sure is a lot of work involved, more than I

thought." Isabella watched the screen of Jim and Harry in the King Street room and pointed to the antique maple desk that stood in front of the windows. "I just saw a shadow zip by the window. Did you see that?"

"Yes, I did, but that was a car's headlights, but that's okay, you're alert. One of the main things we try to do is debunk anything that can be explained." Marie smiled and continued to watch the monitor.

Gale asked, "Isabella, getting back to our earlier conversation about those symbols. Have you ever read *The Gold Bug*?"

"No, I haven't, but I plan on it. I remember asking my mom what the big deal was with Poe's Tavern and the Poe library. She just said that Edgar Allan Poe wrote that book when he lived here." Isabella looked at Marie and asked, "Do you think there's buried treasure here?"

"I don't know. The practical side of me says no, but who's to say?"

Isabella wiggled back in the folding canvas stool and asked, "What is the history of Poe at Sullivan's Island anyway? Was he really here?"

Marie replied, "I don't know all of the details, but he was here in the late eighteen twenties. He enlisted into the army and was stationed here at Fort Moultrie. He didn't write *The Gold Bug* until eighteen-forty something."

"Wow, I actually thought it was all legend that he was at Sullivan's Island. I think I'll go to the library soon and get the book."

Gale said, "I think the team wants to read it again also. We need to understand all of the symbols you wrote down."

The radio cracked and Harry's voice softly came over the speaker. "Command central, are you seeing any fluctuations on the laser grid in the Maverick suite?"

Marie pushed the button in on the radio and softly said, "I do see a little movement there Harry. I'll be sure to mark it here. Maybe you can use the recorders and ask a few questions to see if you get any response."

"Copy that. We both sensed the room changed a little. It feels a lot colder than it was."

Gale pointed to where Jim stood against the mustard painted wall and said, "There seems to be a little movement next to Jim through the laser grid. Can either of you see it? Look at the changes of the grid line on the antique dresser."

"Oh yeah, I can see it." Isabella excitedly sat straight up and pointed at the monitor. "It was pretty subtle, but I think I saw it."

Marie grabbed the notebook and began to take notes. She marked the time of the fluctuation and then pushed the button to speak to Jim. "Good catch you guys. I've marked the time in our notebook. We'll be sure to pay attention to our analysis. Let's hope we've also caught something on our recorders. Let's go another fifteen minutes and then change up positions. I'd like to take Isabella to the Queen Street room. There were a lot of claims in that area."

Isabella smiled, stood up, then swayed against Gale and sat back down. "I just saw the headless spirit again. He's over there against the corner of the van. He's making me dizzy."

Gale jumped out of the way and said, "Whoa,

where is he? Is he behind me? I hate when they do that."

Marie looked toward the corner and telepathically asked him to reveal himself normally. "It's okay. You need to remember to tell him to look normal when he appears. Although, I suspect he gets a kick out of scaring you. Are you alright?"

"Yeah, I'm fine. Is it normal to get dizzy?"

"Yes, it is, and sometimes you'll feel how they feel. There's obviously a reason why he's appeared, and now he knows I'm able to communicate with him also. Why don't we try and see what he wants?"

Isabella looked toward the same corner and asked, "What do you want? Why are you here?"

Marie started to speak when her cell phone vibrated in her pocket. She pulled it out and said, "I just got a text from Cory. They found another body."

Gale's eyes grew large as she slumped against the small table. "I guess we know why the headless dude is here."

Isabella looked back at the corner and said, "He's gone."

Marie heard Tim yell from outside of the van. "Gale, can you open up? I've got to go. I just got paged. Apparently, there's been another body found on Folly Beach. We agreed to keep each of our department's up-to-speed when anything new developed."

Gale opened the door, stepped down from the van, and wrapped her arms around Tim. "Yeah, Cory just texted Marie, and we had another visit from our headless friend. What the hell is going on? Please be careful, okay? Keep in touch."

Tim softly kissed the top of Gale's head and then winked. "Roger that, I'll see you later."

. . .

CORY STOOD next to Sergeant Peter McMillan of the Folly Beach Police Department as they watched the emergency crew dressed in wetsuits and swim fins pull the harnessed dead body from the ocean and drag it further onto the beach. Cory received a courtesy call an hour earlier in the middle of his third cup of coffee.

Sergeant McMillan wiped the sweat from his brow with the back of his hand and returned his hat to the top of his balding gray head. He was a foot shorter and broader than Cory with narrow stern green eyes that were tired with age from the many years of being on the force and witnessing dead bodies.

The bloated body was covered with blisters and had turned a greenish black. There were noticeable pieces of flesh eaten away by the ocean's fish population. Cory covered his nose from the stench and grudgingly walked with McMillan to join their ME. As with the other bodies, the victim was male and missing a head.

Cory walked in step with McMillan and cringed as he got closer to the body. He nodded at the pencil-thin gentleman with chestnut hair wearing *Where's Waldo* glasses. "Hello, my name's Chief Miller. I take it you're the medical examiner. What's your estimated time of death?"

The ME casually looked up at Cory and McMillan and flatly stated, "Brilliant deduction on the ME part, my name is Gerard Butler, and no, I'm not related to the actor. The ocean deterioration has made the determination of death a bit difficult. I won't be able to give you an exact time of death until I examine the body back in my lab."

Cory's right eyebrow rose as he glanced over at McMillan and then gave his attention back to the flippant ME. "Yes, I can *clearly* see the deterioration of the body, but why don't you try and give us a guesstimate?"

McMillan raised his hand before the ME spoke and said, "Gerry, let's cut to the chase. It's two in the morning, and I'm really not in the mood for your smart-ass comments. You can give us an idea of how long the body was in the ocean. A week? A month?"

Gerard jammed his glasses up the bridge of his nose and pointed to the blisters on the shoulders. "Given the fact that there is presence of grave wax and blisters all over the body, along with the discoloration, I would estimate this body has been in the ocean for about three weeks. In case you're wondering, grave wax is where the tissues have turned into a soapy fatty acid."

"Thank you. I'm familiar with what grave wax is." Cory turned his attention to McMillan and said, "I think we can agree this is another victim with the same MO as the others. I'd appreciate any results you get from the full report."

"Absolutely, and I apologize for Gerry's rude response. He tends to get territorial with his bodies." McMillan chuckled and slapped his hand on Gerry's back. "Isn't that right Gerry?"

Gerry grimaced and said, "You'll have my full report in a couple of days."

Cory nodded. "Thank you, I appreciate it. Pete, just exactly what's your take on these murders? This is the third body we've found with the heads chopped off, and the second one found on your beach."

"I don't know, and as much as I hate to say the words, serial killer, I think that's what we've got on our hands."

Gerry smugly added, "I think the correct term is severed or decapitated."

"Yeah, I kind of like the words chopped off." Cory shook his head and turned with McMillan as they walked toward their vehicles. "I thought my ME was a little uptight."

McMillan heartily laughed and jammed his hat down on his head. "You have no idea, my friend. You have no idea."

TEN

MARIE QUICKLY YANKED the covers over her head to keep her eyes from watering from the glare of the sun when she felt Cory carefully lean against her and drape his arm over her waist. "Is it morning already? What time is it?"

Cory said, "It's not morning anymore. From what I can make out on the clock it is officially noon."

"Noon, holy crap I wanted to go into the office. I have a ton of paperwork to finish." Marie abruptly turned toward Cory and smiled. "Hello there, my husband, I don't remember hearing you come home. Come to think of it, I'm surprised Bailey didn't hear you. What time did you get in?"

"A little after three and you were completely out when I got into bed. So was Bailey."

Marie looked over Cory's shoulder at Bailey lying on his side dead to the world. "Yeah, he had an eventful night investigating."

"Speaking of which, how was it at the Post House?"

"It was amazing. We had a ton of activity. We'll have our work cut out for us on our analysis. Dayna was a great host. I just hope we were able to capture enough to give her some answers. We all had a lot of personal experiences." Marie ran her hand through Cory's thick brown hair and asked, "How about you? Was the body you found headless?"

"Oh yeah and covered in blisters with a cool greenish-black shade about him."

"Him? So, it was another male victim? And he was covered in blisters?" Marie squirmed under the covers and nuzzled her head under his chin.

"Why is it Mrs. Miller, we end up having these gory conversations in the mornings either before or during breakfast?"

"I guess it's just part of our world." Marie felt the bed bounce as Bailey jumped up and wiggled his way between them. "Look who decided to join the living. Good morning, Bailey, I suppose you are ready to go out?"

"From the way his tail is wagging, I'd say that's a yes." Cory shifted himself from the center of the bed, slipped on his jeans, and grabbed a shirt. "Come on boy, let's go and get some fresh air. We'll let mommy start the coffee."

"I'll take that deal. My legs are sore from swimming the other day. Not to mention my back is stiff from sitting on that stupid stool in the van last night." Marie swung her legs to the side of the bed and twisted her hair into a makeshift ponytail. "So, before we get busy with our day, were there any other details about the body?"

"No, I'll have to wait for the report from their ME, who by the way was a real pompous ass."

"Really and why do you say that?"

"Because he looked like Waldo and corrected my

grammar." Cory opened the bedroom door with Bailey in tow.

"Hey, nobody corrects my man. I'd have punched him square in the nose." Marie stood up and kissed Cory's cheek.

"I would have liked to have seen that because I think you could have taken him down." Cory winked and followed Bailey out of the bedroom.

Marie quickly slipped one of Cory's oversized T-shirts over her head and followed them into the kitchen. "You'd better believe it, wait how big was this guy?"

"Trust me, one of your spirit guides could have taken this guy down." Cory slid into his running shoes and attached the leash to Bailey's collar and said, "We'll be back just in time for breakfast."

"Wait a minute. I thought I was only making coffee." Marie stuck out her lip and shrugged. "It's not working, is it? Yeah, it doesn't work when Gale does it either. Okay, toast it is, and I'll even get out the strawberry jam."

"What a way to a man's heart, nothing better than toast and jam." Cory patted Bailey's side and let the door close behind him.

Marie yelled, "And coffee, don't forget I'm also making coffee."

Isabella walked into the kitchen wearing sweatpants and a Moultrie Middle School Junior Achievement T-shirt. Her hair was tangled in her elastic hair tie, and she only wore one sock. She opened the refrigerator and grabbed the gallon of milk and nearly dropped it when she turned around and spotted the headless spirit lingering in the corner of the kitchen.

"Okay, you need to stop doing that. Please put

your head back on. I've asked you that countless times. Why is that so difficult for you to remember?" Isabella sat down in the kitchen chair and shook her head. "I seriously can't believe I'm talking to you. Is there a reason why you're here again? You disappeared so fast last night. Apparently, they found another headless body. Did you know something about that too?"

Before Isabella could switch to a higher frequency and listen to the headless spirit, Adam walked into the kitchen, and the spirit vanished. "Oh man, you just scared Henry away, but I think I was able to get what he said before he disappeared again."

Adam's eyebrows went up and asked, "Who?"

"Henry...the headless spirit."

"His name is Henry?"

"I don't know, but that's what I call him. Henry the headless guy, it just made sense to me." Isabella set the milk on the table and then grabbed a box of cereal from the cupboard. "He came to us last night in the van on our investigation. Then he disappeared right after Marie got a text that they found another headless dead body on Folly Island."

"This stuff creeps me out. How can being able to see and talk to a dead guy not freak you out? Especially one without a head? So, what did *Henry* say?"

Isabella took a clean bowl from the dishwasher, began to fill it with cereal, then sat down across from Adam. "I think he said something that sounded like Bishop Hotel, and I guess I'm not afraid anymore because Marie explained they're no different from people that are alive. In fact, they're probably easier to deal with. Besides, I like helping. For whatever reason, Henry has chosen to use me to communicate with instead of Marie. So, if I can help out with these murders, then I think it's cool."

"Yeah well, Mom doesn't think it's cool. I mean, she supports you and all, but I think it still upsets her that you can do this."

"I know, but she'll come around." Isabella poured the milk into the bowl, shoved a spoonful of cereal into her mouth and chewed for a few seconds then asked, "How do you feel about it? Do you support me?"

Adam slouched back into the chair and said, "Yeah I do, because then they leave me alone. So, what do you think Bishop Hotel means?"

MARIE STARED at the file on Chappie, the Miller's French bulldog, and tried to concentrate on filling out the paperwork for his release for a routine surgery to replace his tear gland. So many thoughts slipped in and out of her mind about the murders. Beetles being shoved down a man's throat, headless victims, Isabella being sought out by one of the victim's spirit instead of her, their latest ghost investigation, organizing the retreat for kids with psychic abilities, and not to mention she hadn't heard from Myra. As soon as she slipped the paperwork back into the file, she felt a chill run up her spine. In the past, she would have cast it aside, but she knew all too well she was about to encounter a spirit.

She took a deep breath, cleared her mind, and began to feel warm as she smiled and said, "Hello Myra, I was just thinking about you as I'm sure you're aware. You know I don't like dealing with these murders and making decisions without your help."

Myra appeared in a white glow and eventually formed into what Marie remembered her before she crossed over. "You need to continue to trust yourself, Marie. You're making good decisions."

"I know, I do trust myself most of the time, but now that Isabella is being approached by one of the dead victims, it makes me nervous. I'm sure she's more open and easier to contact, but she's also still learning about her ability. I don't want it to overwhelm her."

"You must continue the teachings I gave you. It will help her to control her ability. Her angels are with her, as I am. You need to meditate more Marie."

Before Marie could continue the conversation, Myra disappeared. "Myra, why do you leave before I'm finished asking you questions? Like, who's committing all these murders? Okay, I know it doesn't work that way. You only appear when I let my thoughts consume me too much, which keeps me off guard. I guess it's time to wrap things up here and go home to meditate. I need to focus better."

Marie's cell phone rang, and she read Isabella's name as she tapped the phone to answer. "Hi Isabella, did you get enough sleep after our investigation? He did? No, I'm not sure I know what Bishop Hotel means, but why don't we ask the team when we meet this evening to go over our analysis? Great, I'll see you at six."

Marie slipped the phone into the pocket of her sweater and continued to make some final notes before checking with the veterinarian on-call to be sure the overnight guests received their needed medicine. She wasn't sure what Bishop Hotel meant, but she needed to call Gale to remind her to bring *The Gold*

Bug with her this evening. It was time to pull everyone's knowledge and opinions about Isabella's cryptic messages.

IT WAS the usual scenario of the team sitting at their stations reviewing countless hours of video and audio recordings in the upper room over Marie's garage. Most of the team had re-read *The Gold Bug,* and they agreed to discuss the story at the end of the analysis.

Harry raised his hand while tapping on his headphones to get someone's attention. "I think I have a very interesting audio clip here. I'd like someone else's opinion on it."

Jim ran his hands through his thinning hair, leaned over, and took the headphones from Harry. "I'll take a listen."

Harry said, "Pay attention when you see the clock hit twenty-two point eighteen."

Jim watched the clock and when it reached the appropriate time he jumped and then removed his headphones. "If I'm hearing correctly, I think the voice answered yes right after Mimi asked if they wanted us to leave."

"That's exactly what I heard. I'm going to mark it and add this to the analysis tape for Dayna."

Marie stood up and stretched her back and then looked around the room. "Is everyone about finished with his or her sections? I've gone through everything that I had." After seeing everyone's head nod in unison, she said, "Great, why don't we finish up, take a few minutes to regroup, have some snacks, and then come back to chat about Isabella's encounters and the cryptogram."

Isabella said, "Good ol' Henry."

Harry asked, "What encounters, and who is Henry?"

Isabella laughed and said, "Sorry, I named the dead headless guy Henry. I'm not sure why, but it seemed to fit."

Gale said, "Cory learned his name is James Lawson."

"It is? Gee, I've been calling him Henry. I wasn't aware of his name."

"That's okay; I don't think it matters."

"Maybe, but I think I should call him by his correct name."

Marie said, "Yes, I need to fill you all in on the latest information. Cory said it was okay to share this with everyone. Dr. Brasher found a counterfeit hundred-dollar bill, and a beetle shoved down Skerrett's throat, which is what actually killed him. Lawson, our second victim, had his hands chained together, almost as if it was a punishment. We then learned that Isabella is now being visited by Lawson."

Jim replied, "Wow, now that *is* interesting."

"We can discuss more after we have all of our sections marked on the final tape for Dayna. I'd like to have Jim and Harry create a master, but first I need to take Bailey out for a few minutes." Marie chuckled when Bailey lifted his head, and his ears stood up.

Isabella smiled as Bailey walked over and knocked papers off the table with his tail. "He's such a great dog. I can't believe how in-tune he is to ghosts. He was amazing at the investigation."

Marie snapped the leash onto Bailey's collar and rubbed Bailey's ears. "Yeah, he is a great dog. He responded really well to all of the training Myra and I gave him to go on investigations. He picks up on spirit before any of us can."

Isabella grabbed a chocolate chip cookie and said, "I'll go with you. I need some fresh air."

"Okay, I'd love the company."

Marie held onto Bailey's leash and tried to keep from being pulled down the stairs headfirst. "He can be a monster when he goes for a walk. He may do great on investigations, but he still gives me fits when he doesn't listen and heel."

"I wish I had a dog. We're not allowed in our condo." Isabella watched Bailey lift his leg and add his DNA to the sand and said, "Marie, what do you think the team is going to say to these visits I'm getting from Lawson?"

"How do you mean?"

"They're not going to think I'm crazy?"

Marie firmly held Bailey's leash, turned to Isabella, and said, "Absolutely not, they've been dealing with me for the past three years. They know you have a gift, Isabella, so don't worry about it, okay? Now come on, let's get back to the team and try to see if we can't help solve these murders."

After everyone had taken a break, they began poring through copies of *The Gold Bug* as Marie stood at the whiteboard writing down comments, thoughts, and opinions of what Isabella's cryptograms meant, as well as the Bishop Hotel.

Tim spoke without looking up as he continued to read the Poe book. "We all know that the cryptogram pointed Legrand, the main character in the story, to where Captain Kidd's treasure was buried."

Harry wiped his brow with his forearm and took a sip of water. "We also know the Bishop Hotel was another word for hostel. I believe the old family Bessop was supposed to represent a large rock near the Bessop's Castle. Legrand sat on the rock and was able to look through a telescope and use the coordinates that were in that cryptogram to find where the treasure was buried."

Tim rubbed his eyes and said, "Yeah that's right, I remember the story better now. But was there ever a family on the island named Bishop or Bessop?"

Jim replied, "I think all of this is fiction. I don't believe there was a family with those names here on the island."

"Then why did Lawson tell me that?" Isabella slouched down into the chair and folded her arms firmly on her chest.

"Isabella, don't get discouraged. It doesn't mean this isn't significant. It's just a matter of organizing all of this information and working together to find an answer. When you and I receive messages, they're a bit cryptic." Marie looked at Mimi. "Were you able to find anything in the documents with the historical society?"

"Nothing that stands out about Isabella's meet-up with Lawson and what he's told her. Most of it is folklore after the story was published. I think I remember hearing stories from the older locals that people thought there was buried treasure on the island. Others have said it was already found."

"Okay, so why cut off the head and then shove a beetle and money down his throat? What significance does that have to the story?" Gale grabbed a mirror from her purse and began touching up her lipstick.

"I don't know. That's the same thing I wondered. Does that have something to do with my vision about the headless skeletons on Folly Island? They're finding bodies there too and why were Lawson's hands chained together?" Marie rubbed her temples and tried to relax her shoulders by pushing them hard against the chair.

Tim said, "I forgot about that part. Personally, I don't think it has anything to do with the story. I agree with Cory and that someone tortured him for a reason."

Isabella jumped at Bailey barking as her eyes grew wide. She shivered and pointed to the corner of the room. "Everyone, it looks like Bailey is spot on again. Lawson's hovering over in the corner of the room by the coffee pot."

ELEVEN

CORY SAT in his office and tried to keep his eyes focused as he read the coroner's report on the latest John Doe. The Folly Island Police Department came up with no results on the fingerprints to identify the body. It had been two weeks, and they weren't any closer to solving the murders.

Cory looked up at Tom walking in with a big grin on his face. "I hope that grin has something to do with this case and not because you won the latest office pool of how many ghost peppers Bull can eat in a minute."

"We had to stop taking those bets; Bull is on medication for acid reflux. I *am* grinning about a lead I just got on our second victim." Tom sat down in the adjacent chair and pulled out his notebook. "I finally tracked down an inmate who shared a cell with Lawson. His name's Benjamin Beach, a.k.a. King Kong and he's looking for a plea bargain. Charleston's Special Investigation Unit just hauled him in for possession of cocaine around a school with the intent to sell. He says he knows some information on Lawson's dealings outside of prison and a particular conversation he had with him about counterfeiting. I asked them to keep him in holding until we can talk to him."

Cory shoved out of his chair and grabbed his hat. "What are we waiting for, let's head over there? This is the first real lead we've had, great work Tom."

MARIE STOOD FROZEN as she watched Lawson move back and forth in the corner of the room. "Isabella, I can see him too. Why don't you try to communicate with him? Ask simple questions."

"I'll try, but sometimes I have a hard time understanding what he says." Isabella took a deep breath and tried to focus. "Why are you here? I said why are you here? You're not making any sense. What does Bishop Hotel mean? Has it got anything to do with buried treasure? Why were your hands chained together? Do you know who killed you?"

"That's good, is he giving you any answers?" Marie slowly walked over to Isabella and stopped short. "Oh, he's gone."

Isabella slumped down into the chair and dropped her head into her hands. "This stuff really wears me out."

"Gale please get her some water." Marie sat next to Isabella and said, "You need to take deep breaths and just relax. It does wear you out. You have to be careful not to let it drain you."

Isabella took the glass of water from Gale, gulped it down, and then leaned back in the chair. "I had a hard time understanding him. I haven't mastered that whole frequency thing, but I did manage to get a yes when I asked about the buried treasure. I also think he said something about betrayal. I don't know. It was all jumbled together."

"You did fantastic, Isabella, really you did. I was able to get a little more regarding the betrayal. He said he betrayed someone. I think that's the reason he was murdered, which does make sense why his hands were chained together."

"I think maybe you and Isabella need to talk with Cory in an official capacity. This is a little more information than what they've had to this point." Tim took Isabella's glass and set it by the coffee pot. "Didn't you say he was supposed to get the autopsy report on the third victim?"

"Yes, he's at the station now. I can text him to see if we can come over and fill him in on this latest visit, but in the meantime, I think we need to continue dissecting this story to see if that takes us anywhere."

Mimi said, "I'm going to see if I can get more information at the library tomorrow. They're closed today. Genevieve is quite a Poe fan. She may be able to shed some light on this also."

"I think that's a great idea, Mimi." Marie looked at Jim and asked, "Can you and Harry finalize this analysis for Dayna? I need to take Isabella home after we meet with Cory. Let me know when you've finished, and I'll contact her about when we can go over the findings."

"Sure, not a problem, we've got everything narrowed down."

Gale walked over to the table of snacks and began clearing the dishes. "Tim and I can clean this up and watch Bailey. You go ahead and see if any of this information can help with the case. We also need the team to discuss a few of the requests we received from our psychic kids website."

"That's right we need to talk about our psychic kids retreat. We have three families interested in coming here for some guidance. We weren't expecting such a quick response. Let's coordinate our schedules to meet and discuss when we can have these families visit." Marie felt her phone vibrate and read the text message from Cory. "It looks like Cory got a lead on the case. He and Tom are interviewing someone who supposedly shared a jail cell with Lawson. Isabella, we'll share this with Cory later, I think I need to take you home now."

Harry asked, "I was wondering, since the first and second victims were in the same prison, do you think this latest victim was too? There seems to be some commonality between these men."

"I don't know, but hopefully we'll soon find out." Marie walked over to Isabella and draped her arm over her shoulder. "Why don't I take you home now? It's been a long day, and I'll be sure to fill you in on what Cory finds out at the prison. We need to ask your mom if she'll allow you to meet with Cory and if she minds you helping with these murders."

THE CHARLESTON POLICE DEPARTMENT, located on Broad Street, was a stately looking building made of concrete and marble. There were staircases with wrought iron railings on the left and right sides of the building that met in the middle of the front door.

Cory and Tom walked into the station and were greeted at the front desk by the lieutenant of the day.

The tall, blond-haired, authoritative-looking gentleman glanced up and said, "Can I help you?"

Cory didn't recognize the lieutenant and pulled out his ID and said, "I'm Chief Cory Miller from the Sullivan's Island Police Department. My deputy, Tom Simmons, talked with someone regarding a drug supplier brought in for cocaine possession with intent to sell. He's apparently got some information about our murder investigation. He claims to have shared a cell with our second victim, James Lawson."

The lieutenant looked down the call sheet and said, "Yeah, here it is. He's in holding room three. The officers that brought him in are Bates and Hancock. I'll buzz you in, just head down the hall to the right."

Cory placed his wallet back into his pants pocket and nodded his head. "Thanks, I appreciate it."

They heard the buzz and the locked door released as Cory grabbed the handle to enter the sealed off precinct. He saw the hall and proceeded to walk with Tom toward holding room three all the while taking in the sounds of distant yelling, phones ringing, fingers tapping on computers, and the whirring of a copy machine.

Tom pointed to the small metal plaque marked *Holding #3* and said, "This is it. How do we want to play this?"

Cory peered through the interior blinds on the window and said, "It looks like Bates and Hancock are in there with the perp. There's a woman in a suit, so we can guess she's from the DA's office. We don't have to agree to anything. It pisses me off this guy is back in again for intent to sell cocaine around a school. Let's see what he has for us, and as Marie always says, let it up to the universe to decide his fate."

Tom nodded and waved his hand toward the door. "After you."

Cory opened the door, looked around the room, and landed his eyes on a slim plain-clothes cop leaning against the wall holding a hot cup of coffee with a cigarette dangling between his lips. He looked to be in his forties with long straggly brown hair and a scruffy three-day beard. The other cop was seated and resting his arms on the back of a chair. He too was in plain clothes with short black hair and a mustache styled from the nineties. They looked like they had stepped out of the movie *Lethal Weapon*.

The woman stood in high-heeled pumps wearing a form fitted navy suit with long blonde hair tied back in a loose ponytail. She slid her glasses to the top of her head and extended her hand and said, "Hello, I'm Jenny Steel from the DA's office, nice to meet you."

Cory shook her hand and said, "I'm Chief Cory Miller from Sullivan's Island, and this is my deputy, Tom Simmons."

The cop with the coffee stood up and said, "I'm Officer Dave Bates, and this is my partner, John Hancock."

John grimaced and said, "Yeah, I get that look all the time. Not sure what my parents were thinking when they named me."

Cory smiled and proceeded to stand directly in front of the perp and folded his arms against his chest. The huge man sitting in the chair wearing handcuffs had dark hairy arms and knuckles. Cory said, "And this must be our friendly cocaine dealer."

Jenny grabbed the file on the table and pulled out the arrest report. "This is Mr. Benjamin Beach, a.k.a. King Kong. He was picked up for possession of cocaine at C. E. Williams Middle School on Butte Street. This is his second offense."

Bates set his coffee cup down on the table and grinned at King Kong. "Kong here seems to think he has some information regarding these beheadings that have taken place on your island and Folly Beach. Isn't that right Kong?"

"That's right, but I ain't sayin' nothin' 'til I know I can cut a deal."

Jenny said, "We can reduce the charges to just possession and remove the intent to sell, but only if Chief Miller is content with the information you have."

Kong said, "Yeah, well I got some good information about these bodies being found without their heads."

Cory sat down in the chair across from King Kong and said, "I'm listening."

"Me and Lawson was sharing a cell while waiting for our trial last January. He was bragging it all up that he had some rich dude gonna pay his bail so he could use his counterfeiting talent." Kong looked around the room and then continued, "He was bragging it up that he was gonna make enough money to retire to the Keys. I asked him what this dude needed the funny money for, and he said to pay for services hunting for buried treasure."

Cory remembered the Poe story but nonchalantly asked, "So what's that got to do with these murders?"

Kong slowly looked at everyone in the room and casually slumped down in his seat. "'Cause Lawson said this guy was one of them really weird dudes that lost his temper if you pissed him off, which Lawson said scared him 'cause he had this big ass sword and that he wasn't afraid to use it. Ain't that a coincidence that Lawson's head was chopped off?"

Cory looked at Tom and then back at Kong. "Mr. Kong, I don't believe in coincidences. Did Lawson say anything more about this *dude*? Was he white, black, tall, or short? Did he have any characteristics or distinguishing marks? Did he say how they met?"

"Nah, Lawson kinda got quiet after he mentioned the sword. Almost like he knew if he said too much, he'd be on the other end of it."

Cory stood up from his chair and said, "Thanks for the information."

"Am I gonna get my deal?"

"We'll see what Ms. Steel wants to do, but this information was helpful. It doesn't give us any real leads, but it coincides with some other details we have." Cory nodded at Bates and Hancock. "Thanks again for allowing us some time here today. Ms. Steele, can I speak with you outside?"

Jenny followed Cory and Tom out of the holding room and closed the door behind them. "How do you want me to proceed?"

"I don't care what you offer. The intel he provided sounds legit regarding our case, but I can't handle letting an ass hole like that off easy for selling drugs to middle school kids."

Jenny smiled and said, "I'm confident the charges are rock solid and that he should go to trial. I have no problem putting him behind bars."

Cory smiled and said, "Sounds good to me. Thanks again, and it was nice meeting you."

Cory left the police station feeling great with the information they learned and keeping a drug dealer off the streets. Now it was time to get with Marie and the SIPS team to match up these facts with *The Gold Bug* and whatever it was Marie needed to share with him about Isabella and the latest visit from the dead headless Lawson.

THE MOON CAST a shadow through the window as the winds picked up bringing in a storm. Marie yawned when she saw it was after ten and slid further into the couch when she caught Bailey's glance and said, "He should be home by now, don't ya think? I take it by your wagging tail you agree with that statement?"

Marie heard the door open and chuckled at Bailey's titled head. "Guess who that is?"

Cory walked around the corner and almost lost his balance when Bailey jumped up and landed his paws on his stomach. "Hello there, boy, were you waiting for me to come home?"

Marie chuckled and said, "Yes, we both were. I poured you a glass of wine. It's over on the dining table. There's also some cheese and crackers I brought back from our meeting."

"I could use a glass of wine. How'd your analysis go? I guess we have quite a bit to talk about with headless Lawson's latest visit." Cory grabbed the glass of wine and popped a cracker into his mouth. He shook his head at Bailey's stare and tossed another cracker in the air as Bailey gracefully caught it in his mouth and swallowed the cracker in one gulp.

"You spoil him." Marie shook her head and then said, "I'm more interested in hearing about your lead at the police station."

Cory threw his hat on the back of the chair and

sat next to Marie on the couch. He wrapped one arm around her shoulders and carefully took a sip of Merlot with the other. He then kissed her on the forehead and filled her in on the conversation King Kong had with Lawson.

"That matches up with mine and Isabella's visions about the sword and the story about the buried treasure from Lawson the other day, which we know isn't a coincidence. However, none of it makes sense. I don't believe there's any buried treasure here on the island, and why did I have a vision of those bodies found back in nineteen eighty-seven on Folly Beach? Or is it really about those bodies?"

"I'm not sure, but whoever hired Lawson to do the counterfeiting must be a little crazy. According to Kong, Lawson was scared of him, and for good reason."

Marie asked, "By the way, why is he called King Kong?"

"I'm guessing because he has hairy knuckles."

"Okay, fair enough." Marie took the last sip of wine and set the glass on the end table. She slipped her foot out from Bailey's side and brought it up under her on the couch. "To answer your earlier question, our analysis went really well. We have some great stuff to show Dayna, but the reason Isabella and I were going to meet you at the station was because Lawson showed up again, and this time I was able to hear what he was saying. We were able to figure out that he *did* betray someone, which is why his wrists were chained, but what that betrayal is, we have no idea. Oh, and he confirmed that his previous cryptic message is about buried treasure."

"I still haven't heard anything more from the ME

on our third victim. With as much damage that was done to the body from the ocean, not sure what they'll be able to find."

"The team suspects this victim was in prison with Lawson and Skerrett too. Before I forget, we're going to get together to chat later this week about the responses to the blog for our psychic kids retreat. I'm going to have Isabella be a part of that too. I think it'll help her to gain the confidence she needs if she can help other kids."

"I think this is a great thing you're putting together. Myra would be proud." Cory sat up and sternly looked at Marie and said, "I've wanted to ask you a question, but I hesitate to do so because I know how worn out you can get using some of your abilities."

"You want me to use my psychometry on the counterfeit hundred, don't you?"

Cory's eyebrows went up, and a slow smile fell across his face. "Did you just read my mind?"

"Actually, no I didn't, but I thought of the same thing. I think it's a great idea. It's helped us in the past." Marie sat up on the edge of the couch and stretched her back. "Why don't I talk with Isabella to find a good time for us to come over to the station? Her mom is more than okay with her helping us out. While we're there, I can see if I pick up anything on the money."

Cory grabbed Marie's chin and gently stroked her cheek with his thumb. "Thank you. In the meantime, why don't we call it a day? I'm exhausted."

"I am too, I had different thoughts earlier this evening for when you came home, but I may have to postpone those until the morning."

Cory pulled Marie tight against his chest and softly kissed her neck. "I had those same thoughts."

Chills fluttered down Marie's neck as she closed her eyes. "If we're in agreement to wait until the morning, you need to stop kissing my neck."

Cory chuckled and pulled back to look Marie in the eyes. "You have a way of putting a spell on me Mrs. Miller."

"Gee, and I wasn't even trying."

Cory grabbed Marie's hand as they walked toward the bedroom. "I think we need to leave Bailey out here so we can have some privacy."

TWELVE

ADAM AWOKE to the sound of Isabella's voice talking in the night. He walked into his sister's room and stopped short as Isabella continued to stare and talk to the wall. He watched her animated gestures and chose to remain quiet until he felt it was safe to approach her. He knew she was talking to headless Henry.

He saw Isabella slump down onto her bed and immediately walked over and sat down next to her. "Are you okay?"

Isabella slowly looked at Adam as a tear slipped down her cheek. "I'm okay."

"Then why are you crying? Were you talking to headless Henry?"

"His name is James Lawson, and yes I was, and I don't know why I'm crying."

Adam pulled Isabella toward him and carefully stroked her back. "Isabella, I don't like when this happens to you. It scares me. I'm supposed to be your big brother, and I can't even protect you from any of this. If something happened, you can tell me."

Isabella smiled at her brother and slid back under

the covers. "I'm exhausted. Can we talk about this in the morning? I promise I'll tell you everything."

He smiled and kissed his sister on the forehead. "Okay, go back to sleep."

As he walked toward the door, he turned to stare at Isabella. He knew his sister was keeping something from him. She was a terrible liar. He had a sneaky suspicion she had no plan of telling him what happened. He could read her expression. Whatever it was, it had her scared, which made him angry. He didn't like anyone messing with his sister...dead or alive.

MARIE SHOVED a piece of toast in her mouth and balanced it between her teeth as she poured coffee into her travel mug. She snapped the lid tight and saw Bailey longingly look at her while his tail wagged in excitement. "Okay, okay I'm getting your dog food. Don't make me feel any more guilty for making you sleep out here." She poured the dog food into his dish and whispered in Bailey's ear. "It was his fault."

Cory turned the corner and said, "Whose fault?"

"Nothing, just a little something personal between Bailey and me."

"You're blaming me for making him sleep in the living room, aren't you?"

"What, would I do something like that?" Marie chuckled and continued to finish her toast. "I'm in a hurry to get to the clinic. Can you take him out for me?"

"Yeah, no problem, I have a little time this morning." Cory poured coffee into a mug and dropped a spoonful of sugar and slowly stirred the java. "When are you and Isabella coming to the station today?"

"She just texted me and said she'd be done with her tennis lesson by three, so shortly after that. I should be done with my rounds by then." Marie stepped into the powder room and began brushing her teeth. After a few touches with her makeup, she walked back into the kitchen, grabbed her purse and coffee, and rubbed Bailey's head. "I'll see you later. Let me know if you hear anything from the ME on this latest victim."

Cory leaned into Marie and quickly kissed her puckered lips. "I'll let you know as soon as I know. Are you sure you're okay with the psychometry?"

"I'm more than okay." Marie ran out the door and waved and jumped into her black suburban. She opened the window and yelled, "Be sure Bailey has enough water, but not too much. See you after three."

Cory nodded his head and waved. He walked back into the kitchen and saw Bailey looking back at him. "Okay, boy, let's go for your morning constitutional. I need to head to the station."

He leaned over and struggled with the leash as Bailey bumped hard against his legs and shoved his snout under Cory's chin. Cory opened the door and took in a deep breath of fresh ocean air as he walked with Bailey down the back deck stairs and headed toward the beach. Within a few minutes, Bailey did what was needed as Cory cleared the deposit with a baggy. He carefully placed the bag in the garbage when his cell phone rang.

"Yeah Tom, what ya got? I'll be right over. It sounds like there is a connection with these victims. See you in a few." Cory disconnected and led Bailey back to the house. He hoped Marie's psychometry could help them connect the dots.

. . .

MARIE GUIDED Isabella through the station and headed toward Cory's office. She saw Cory wave them in and said, "He's ready for us. All you need to do is relax and share everything you remember about your visions with Lawson."

Isabella followed Marie into Cory's office and sheepishly smiled, "I'll try my best."

Marie leaned forward and quickly kissed Cory's cheek and then directed Isabella to sit down next to her. "I think we're ready to help in any way we can."

"That's great, and thank you both for coming in." Cory reclined back in his office chair and pointed to the corner outside his office. "Would either of you like any coffee or soda? I can have Tom bring something in."

Isabella shook her head. "No, I'm fine, thank you."

"I wouldn't mind a cup of tea." Marie winked and stood up. "I can get it myself, no need to bother anyone. Why don't you have Isabella share with you what she's been able to understand from Lawson first, and then I'll try my psychometry?"

"That sounds like a plan."

Marie walked out of the office and slowly took in her surroundings. She had a quick flashback of being here when Davy McGee aka John Mullican tried to hang her. That was the beginning of everything for her psychic abilities and the SIPS team. She certainly hoped she could help with *this* case.

Marie dangled the tea bag in the plastic cup and re-entered Cory's office. "I see you have decaffeinated green tea now, thank you for that."

Cory smiled and said, "You're welcome. We're

finished with Isabella's statement. She did a great job of remembering the details."

"That's great. You'd be surprised how this can help." Marie sat down in the adjacent chair and slowly took a sip of tea. "Am I up next?"

"Yes, I'm waiting for Larry to bring the evidence bag in here, along with some gloves. Before we get into that, I did want to share with you what I got back from the Folly Island ME." Cory opened the folder that was in front of him and picked up the top sheet. "They were able to match fingerprints with the third victim to a Freddie Stuart. He was in the system because he was a prison guard. You'll never guess which prison he worked in?"

Marie said, "The same prison that Lawson and Skerrett were in?"

Cory tapped his finger on his nose. "Very good deduction my dear Watson."

Isabella giggled and said, "So you think these three guys were somehow involved with each other?"

"It's looking that way, but we're still trying to connect the dots how and why all three were beheaded. I hope with what Marie can do with her psychometry on the counterfeit hundred, it may shed some light on the connection."

Isabella looked at Marie and said, "I googled psychometry. Are you really able to touch things and pick up on the energy?"

"Yes sometimes, and other times it's nothing but a big blur. I'm able to get snippets of information that come to me like images from a movie. Unfortunately, the images can be very sporadic it's hard to make sense of it, but we'll give it a try."

Cory looked out the office door and signaled to a

squat policeman with gray hair and aging eyes. "Larry, you can bring those in here. Marie will need the gloves. This is Isabella Swanson. She's helping us on the case."

Larry smiled and handed the evidence bag containing the counterfeit hundred to Cory and the latex gloves to Marie and said, "Hello Marie, and it's nice to meet you, Isabella."

"Hi, Larry, and thank you." Marie tugged on the gloves and waved goodbye to Larry as he left the office.

Cory handed the bag to Marie and looked her straight in the eye. "Before you go handling this, I want Isabella to understand how this can affect you at times."

Isabella asked, "How does it affect you?"

"Sometimes I go into a trance when I start to pick up the energy, which can at times really drain me."

"I know what that's like. Will you be okay?"

"She'll be fine, as long as you and I are here." Cory picked up a pen and tablet and handed it to Isabella. "I want you to take down anything Marie says, anything at all, no matter how strange it may seem. I'm going to be right next to her in case I need to bring her out of her trance."

Marie closed her eyes and took in a few deep breaths and then opened the evidence bag and took the counterfeit bill into her hands. The second she began to hold the money between her fingers she saw a flash of light streak across the room, which caused her to jump and slam her back against the chair.

She then saw the flash of a bowl and baby wipes and large envelopes all over a floor. There were gloves and scissors and paper on a table with an ironing board next to some sort of machine. Suddenly she smelled a strange chemical, which caused her head to ache with pressure.

The images faded and Marie began to hear loud laughter ringing in her ears. The image of a face began to appear when she heard the same sound of the sword and a sharp shot across her neck. She awoke to the sound of Cory's voice and felt her shoulders being firmly held in his hands.

"Marie, can you hear me now?" Cory slowly rubbed Marie's arms.

"Yes, I can hear you. That was the strangest experience I've ever had using psychometry."

"Isabella, can you please get her a drink of water?" Cory folded a latex glove around the bill and carefully placed it back into the evidence bag.

Isabella returned with the water and handed the cup to Marie. "That was freaky. Your eyes kept rolling in the back of your head."

"I know, sometimes it's not a pretty sight to watch, but I did see some interesting things." Marie drank some water and placed the cup on Cory's desk. "Did I say anything?"

"You kept repeating the words choking and something about a strange smell." Isabella picked up the tablet and read what she wrote. "Yeah, that was all you said, but that wasn't all that happened."

Cory stroked Marie's cheek with his thumb and said, "You're sure you're okay?"

"Yes, I'm fine. What else happened?"

Isabella said, "While you were in your trance, Lawson showed up."

"You're kidding me? What did he say? Were you able to get anything from him this time?"

"Yes, I was able to make out that the reason he was beheaded was because he didn't remove the counterfeit hundred and beetle from Skerrett's throat. I think someone else choked Skerrett with those things, but Lawson was supposed to take them out after Skerrett was beheaded. That's why *he* got his head chopped off."

"Isabella that's fantastic. Cory, her vision and what I just saw make sense. I need to quickly write this down." Marie grabbed the pen and began writing as she told Cory and Isabella the images that flashed before her eyes. "I couldn't make out the face, but I was witnessing this bill being shoved down a throat and hearing choking noises. I can only assume it was Skerrett."

Cory stood up and sat back in his chair and pulled another file from a tall stack on the side of his desk. "I'm going to go out on a limb and say the bowl, baby wipes, and paper were the products used to make the money. The machine you saw was more than likely a printer or scanner."

Marie picked up her tea and took a sip. "That makes sense, but unfortunately I wasn't able to see any clear faces to help us. I heard the sword and felt the pain in my neck, but does any of this really get us closer to the murderer?"

"Yes, it does, because someone is making this money either where they live or in a small facility. This isn't a big money operation. We'll be able to alert the local businesses to be on the lookout for large bills coming through their company. Now we know why Lawson was murdered and I suspect he's going to help us along the way, thanks to Isabella's connection." Cory set the pen down and looked at Marie and then Isabella. "I'm glad you both came in today. This was a big help. Any small clue can lead us to solve this case. I've got Tom digging up more information on Stuart, but I have a feeling this will begin to tie things together."

"I'm glad we decided to do this. There are times things will psychically begin to come to me after I do this. It will allow me to be more open, so who knows what can happen." Marie stood up from her chair and walked over to Cory and again kissed him on the cheek. "I think it's time I get Isabella home and then I'm going to meet with everyone to discuss our psychic kids."

Cory said, "How do you plan to get them together?"

"We have three families that have daughters with some type of psychic ability. That's what I plan to discuss with the team. We'll need to organize a time that suits for everyone to bring them here for a sort of retreat. It could prove to be a little difficult organizing everyone's calendars, but we'll figure it out."

Isabella said, "I'm excited to be involved too. I hope I can help them as much as you've been helping me."

Marie smiled. "I do not doubt that you will."

Cory stood up and walked over to the door and opened it for Marie and Isabella. "I have no doubt either. Nice to see you again Isabella, and Marie, I'll see you at dinner."

"Yes, but I'm afraid it'll be a quick dinner. Maybe you can get some take-out from Sullivan's Restaurant. I could go for some of their crab stuffed mushrooms."

Cory lifted his hand to his head in a salute. "Sullivan's take-out it is."

THIRTEEN

MARIE ANXIOUSLY WAITED for Mimi and Jim to arrive from the airport with their six guests for the psychic kids' retreat. Organizing the team's and families' schedules proved to be more difficult than they envisioned. The only available weekend was now, which was exciting and nerve-wracking due to the recent murders taking place on the islands. After quite a few long discussions, everyone agreed it might prove to be advantageous to have more people available with psychic abilities. Before they knew it, they organized six plane tickets within a day. Everyone felt Myra's house was the perfect place for the retreat. Her three bedrooms and two and a half bath beach house would suit the arrival of the six guests.

Marie glanced at the applications and tried to remember everyone's names and situations. The first application was from Katie and Jean Roach from Sharpsburg, MD. Katie, age eleven, explained in her email that she was being visited by a little boy named Kenny who died in eighteen eighty-four. She also gets visits from a woman named Dorothy, who may be

Kenny's mother. Dorothy scares Katie. Jean isn't able to understand what's going on with her daughter. She's taken her to doctors to rule out any mental illness. The outbursts in the middle of the night frighten Jean and also cause mother and daughter to argue more than they should. Each is trying to get their relationship back on track. Katie just wants her family to believe in her ability.

Megan and Jennifer Williams from Cascade, Idaho, were the next family. Megan, also eleven, shows signs of being an empath. She can feel other people's feelings and see their aura's. This proves to be difficult because Megan hasn't learned how to turn off this ability, which causes her to become withdrawn and depressed. She always feels the need to help others and takes on their negative or pained emotions. Jennifer's basic reason for taking part in this weekend is to understand what her daughter is dealing with and to learn the tools to help Megan with this ability.

Last, but not least, are Alexi and Max Elliott from Akron, Michigan. Alexi also sees spirits who visit her constantly in the night. Alexi is thirteen, and a little older than the other girls. A little boy too, is visiting her with a scary dead mother. Max tries to understand how his daughter feels, but there's a small part of him that wonders if his daughter is making everything up to get attention.

Marie heard a knock at the door and yelled, "Come on in. I'm in the living room."

A voice said, "It's me, Cheryl."

Marie stood up and walked to the kitchen and waved Cheryl into the house. "Hi, how are you? I'm so glad you're available to help us out this weekend. I know how busy your schedule is. This all happened so fast."

Cheryl pulled a small brown tweed suitcase on wheels into the kitchen and set it right next to the counter. She wore blue jeans and a casual green sweater that matched her eyes, and her ginger shag haircut framed her face. "I'm glad to be a part of this Marie. I think this is a great thing you're doing. I'm looking forward to meeting the families."

"Did you have a chance to review their applications I sent you?"

"Yes, I did, and each of them has their own type of ability, as well as situations. It's pretty obvious the families are concerned. I'll have my work cut out for me with the parents." Cheryl leaned against the counter, pulled out a business card, and handed it to Marie. "If it's okay with you, I'd like to invite Joanie Mitchell to speak with Megan. She too is an empathy, and I think she may be able to teach Megan the tools she needs to learn to control her emotions."

"That's fantastic, thanks for setting that up. Anything we can offer to help these girls is a step in the right direction." Marie saw Gale and Tim at the door and waved them to come inside. "Hey there, you two, you remember Cheryl."

Gale sashayed into the kitchen wearing tight skinny jeans with her usual wedged sandals and a tight white T-shirt advertising *Beardcat's Sweet Shop* located on Middle Street, which recently opened and sold the best gelato. "Hi Cheryl, how are you? It's great having you with us this weekend."

Tim smiled and shifted his USGA golf hat on his head and shook Cheryl's hand. "Thanks for coming."

Gale casually glared at Tim and then strutted

over to the kitchen chair and sat down. "Tim, why don't you take Cheryl's bag upstairs?"

Marie said, "Actually, Cheryl is going to sleep on the pull-out sofa in the study. Tim, it's the second room on the left, across the hall from the parlor. Our guests will occupy the three bedrooms upstairs. I thought it would keep them all close and they could connect better being together."

Cheryl replied, "That's a great idea. Will you be staying here also?"

"At first, I wasn't going to, but I think you and I need to be here during the night, just in case any of the girls experience something that frightens them. I'm going to sleep on a blow-up mattress in the parlor. There's plenty of room for Bailey and me."

Tim returned from the study and said, "Speaking of which, where is Bailey?"

"He's at the house. Cory's bringing him over shortly."

Marie heard a knock at the door and spotted Harry awkwardly standing in his rumpled suit and bow tie. "Harry come in and say hello to Cheryl."

Harry opened the door and shifted his glasses up the bridge of his nose and nodded. "Hello Cheryl, nice to see you again."

Cheryl smiled and patted Harry on the shoulder and instantly pulled her hand back after Harry jumped and landed against the refrigerator. "Oh Harry, I didn't mean to scare you. How are you doing?"

Gale rolled her eyes. "He's always jumpy like that. He doesn't like to be touched. He's our little scared rabbit."

Harry nonchalantly sat down at the table and spoke without lifting his head or making eye contact. "I'm not a scared rabbit. It just caught me off guard."

"I'm sorry Harry. I didn't mean to make you jump." Cheryl pushed her sleeves up to her elbows and shifted her purse on her shoulder.

"Okay, I think everyone's here except for Isabella. She had a few things to take care of at home. I asked if Caroline wanted to come, but she said she's working this weekend." Marie looked at Cheryl and asked, "How have their sessions been going? I know you can't give any details."

"They're coming along really well. Adam shared with me that he has some concern for Isabella. He said she had another encounter with this headless spirit the other night and he felt she was keeping something from him. He said she was crying."

Marie's eyebrows puckered together. "Really, she didn't say anything to me. Maybe we can help her to open up about it this weekend. This may be the perfect venue for that."

Gale looked at her watch. "What time will they be here?"

Marie grabbed a pitcher of iced tea and walked toward the door. "I would say within the next half hour. I've set some snacks for everyone outside in the garden. I thought that would be a nice place to meet and start our discussions. After Cheryl and I learn what these families are looking for about their abilities, I'd like to have them help us investigate Fort Moultrie. Cal has agreed to allow us on the property after hours."

Tim took a bottle of water from the counter,

twisted off the cap, and took a gulp and said, "That should be a great place for an investigation. Even though we've been there twice, we always get new experiences. It's nice to have a connection on the inside to allow us to go there so often."

"I agree." Harry adjusted his crooked bow tie and casually looked out the window.

"I'll be back in a minute. I'm going to take this iced tea outside." Marie walked to the back garden and spotted Cory walking with Bailey. He was still in his uniform, which always made her stomach flutter. "Hello there, husband, thanks for bringing Bailey."

Cory smiled and leaned in to kiss Marie's cheek. "Not a problem. When did you want me to come back and talk about the case with the group?"

"I thought Sunday evening would work well. What do you think? It would give us enough time to help these girls and do a little investigating. They all agreed they'd be glad to see if they could help on this case." Marie bent down and rubbed Bailey's neck and kissed him on the head.

"Any extra help works for me. We can all convene at the SIPS meeting room and try to track the timeline and add any information we know to this point. Has anyone arrived yet?"

"No, but they'll be here soon. Are you going to be okay with me sleeping here?"

"Of course, why wouldn't I?"

Marie scrunched up her nose. "I just thought maybe you'd miss me."

Cory smiled and pulled Marie hard against him and planted a kiss on her lips. "Don't worry. I'll be sure you make it up to me."

Marie wrapped her arms around Cory and grabbed his butt. "I have no problems with that."

"Mrs. Miller, what will the neighbors think?"

"Who cares?" Marie chuckled and saw Mimi pull up into the driveway. "Well, so much for fondling you, there are our guests. Why don't you come over and meet them? Then you can head back to the station."

"I'd be glad to, and then I'll take Bailey's food and water dish inside."

Marie removed the cellophane from the plates of crackers, cheese, and fruit and set them on the wicker table. "Great, let's go give our guests a warm welcome."

Marie took Bailey's leash, grabbed Cory's hand, and walked over to Mimi and Jim's van. The parents and daughters slowly emerged from the van and began gathering their luggage from inside. Marie waved and said, "Hello everyone, it's so great to have you here. I'm Marie Miller, and this is my husband Chief Cory Miller, and this is Bailey."

A girl with straggly dishwater blonde shoulder length hair smiled revealing braces said, "Hi I'm Katie Roach, and this is my mom, Jean."

"Nice to meet you both." Marie smiled at Jean who was petite with bleached blonde hair and wore faded skinny jeans, navy blue flats, and a hoodie.

Jean said, "Thank you so much for organizing this for us. We're pretty excited to be here."

Marie shook Jean's hand. "We're excited too. Did you all have the chance to get to know one another?"

A girl with dark brown hair tied back in a ponytail smiled and said, "Yes, we did. Alexi and I are both seeing dead little boys with their mothers."

A gentleman with the same colored hair with a pear-shaped body wearing sweatpants and a windbreaker said, "My name is Max Elliott, and this is my daughter, Alexi."

"Oh yeah, sorry, forgot to introduce myself." Alexi shrugged her shoulders and giggled with Katie.

"It's nice to meet you both and not a problem, Alexi." Marie walked over to the back of the van and spotted a girl with coal black hair perfectly styled in a short bob haircut lingering behind her mother. "You must be Megan."

Megan smiled and carefully shook Marie's hand. "Yes, and this is my mom, Jennifer."

Marie released Megan's hand and extended it to a tall woman with salt and pepper hair wearing a pair of jeans with tall brown leather riding boots and a blue tweed blazer. "It's nice to meet you, Jennifer. I'm so glad to have you here."

"Thank you. It's nice to meet you also. The temperatures here are a bit warmer than what we have in Idaho."

"Yes, it can get a little warm here, but we do get a nice breeze from the ocean."

Cory grabbed a few suitcases and said, "I'll help carry these inside. Marie, are there any room preferences?"

"No, you can just take them upstairs. Everyone can decide which room they'd like to stay in later. Come along everyone, let's go inside and meet the rest of the team and get you settled." Marie spotted Isabella come around the side of the house. "Isabella you're just in time, why don't you come and meet everyone."

After all of the introductions were made, rooms

were chosen, and snacks were eaten, the group settled outside in the garden and patio area and began to discuss the plans for the long weekend.

Mimi grabbed the notebook and began taking notes of the discussion. "Okay everyone, how do we wish to proceed? Cheryl, do you have any ideas on what the best process would be?"

"Actually, I do, I thought it might be a good idea for today, since we're all settling in, for me and Marie to meet with everyone first and learn about each of the situations. We can keep it a casual and open discussion." Cheryl grabbed her iPad and began adding some notes and then said, "Possibly after that, I can sit with the parents as a group, and then I can meet with each of you one-on-one. How does that sound?"

"I think that'll work well." Marie shifted on the wicker chair and rested her foot on Bailey. "While you're meeting with the parents, maybe I can take the girls and show them some of our investigation equipment. I'd also like to give each of you girls a DVD camera to record your feelings, a bit like doing your own documentary."

Gale stood up from the wooden bench and tugged on Tim's sleeve. "I think this may be a good time for us to head on out and let you all do your thing. We'll be back tomorrow to help begin the set-up for our investigation at the fort."

Tim said, "I think you all have enough to keep you busy for the evening. Gale and I made late dinner arrangements at Poe's Tavern."

Mimi got up from the bench and nodded at Jim. "I think we'll head off also if that's okay with everyone?"

"Sure, that's fine, we felt today was more of an introduction day and getting organized for the rest of the weekend." Marie looked at Isabella. "Isabella, you're more than welcome to sleep with me on this queen blow-up mattress, or would you prefer to go home?"

"No, I'd love to stay. My mom said it wasn't a problem."

Harry grabbed another piece of cheese and said, "I'd best be on my way also. Unless, Cheryl, there was something you would need me to help you in any way."

Cheryl smiled and said, "I think we'll be fine, Harry, but thank you for the offer."

Marie stood in the driveway and waved goodbye. "Thanks, everyone, see you all after breakfast."

Cheryl grabbed her iPad and began typing notes. "Would you all like to join me and Marie in the parlor to chat about what it is you'd like to get out of this weekend?"

Marie followed the group inside and turned toward everyone and said, "Does anyone need anything before we begin?" After everyone shook their heads no, Marie continued, "Then why don't we all take a seat and each of you can relax and let us know what's been going on in your lives."

A few hours had passed, and the group shared their stories. They laughed, cried, and opened their hearts. The dialogue was pleasant, and Marie could sense Megan, Katie, and Alexi were eager to learn how to control their abilities. The girls had discovered a safe zone without judgment, and the parents could feel a connection with their daughters. She also noticed Isabella's confidence growing through her caring words and letting the girls know they weren't alone.

Marie caught Megan yawning and said, "I think we can call it a night. Why doesn't everyone get a good night's sleep? Megan, Katie, and Alexi, you can grab one of these mini-DVD recorders and use it whenever you like. Share your thoughts or anything that goes on during your stay here. You can take it along with you on our investigations. These are your personal cameras, and they're yours to keep."

Megan smiled wide and grabbed one of the recorders. "Oh wow, this is really cool, but doesn't Isabella get one?"

"I already have one, Marie gave me one when we got to investigate a place in Mt. Pleasant."

Katie grabbed a camera and began to inspect the buttons. "Thank you, but I've never used one. Can someone show me how it works?"

Alexi grabbed the last one and pointed to a red button. "This is the on button, and this here is the zoom button. Once you have it where you want it, you push this button here to record."

Jean tucked Katie's hair behind her ear and said, "I can help you learn how to use it. I think it's time we head to bed."

Cheryl said, "Yes I'm ready for some sleep." She tucked her iPad under her arm and walked toward the study. "Goodnight everyone, see you in the morning."

They said their goodnights and dispersed to their chosen rooms. Marie came out of the downstairs bathroom and plugged in the air mattress and watched it begin to inflate. "Isabella, there are a few extra pillows in the closet across from the study. Why don't you bring a few in for us?"

"Sure." Isabella left the room and returned with

two extra bed pillows. "I hope I don't bother you while we sleep. I'm sort of all over the place."

"Don't worry about it; I'm used to Bailey knocking me around." Marie spotted Bailey's head pick up after hearing his name and then roll back over to sleep.

"Isabella, Cheryl shared something with me earlier, and I hope you don't think she broke your confidence."

Isabella shifted her feet and stared at the air mattress. "What do you mean?"

"She said that Adam told her you had another visit from Lawson and that you were crying when you came out of your trance. Is everything okay? Did something happen? You know you can share anything with me. You never know if it's something that can help on the case." Marie guided Isabella to sit down with her on the mattress.

"It wasn't anything. I sometimes get emotional after I see a spirit. I pick up on their feelings."

Marie sensed Isabella's hesitation and decided to let the conversation go for another time. She got up, turned off the lamp, then sat back down on the mattress. "Okay, but if you ever feel the need to talk, you know you can call Cheryl or me, and that means any time of the day or night."

Isabella grabbed the covers and pulled it up to her chin. "Thanks, but I'm okay."

Marie reached over and began to rub Bailey's side when a scream from upstairs had her slamming up into a rigid sitting position. "What on earth was that? Was that one of the girls?"

Isabella got up and turned on the lamp. "It sounded like it."

Within a few seconds, Marie and Isabella were up the stairs and standing in Katie's room. Katie was pointing to the corner of the room and said, "Can you see him? He has no head."

Marie looked to where Katie was pointing and saw headless Lawson willowing in the corner of the room. "We can see him, Katie, it's not just you. All you need to do is ask him to appear to you with his head on. I know that sounds odd, but it works."

Isabella said, "It does Katie."

Before Katie could say anything, Lawson disappeared. "He's gone."

By this time, everyone was standing in Katie's room. Marie turned around and said, "Did anyone else see what Katie saw?" She saw Megan and Alexi shake their heads, and then continued, "Okay, let's all try and get back to bed. Katie, will you be okay?"

"I guess so, but who was that and why didn't he have a head?"

Isabella said, "He's one of the victims from the murders that are taking place here. His name is James Lawson."

Jean pulled Katie against her and frantically said, "I'm not sure I'm comfortable with us getting involved in these murders now. I didn't think my Katie was going to see a headless dead man."

"Mom, I'm okay, it just scared me at first that's all." Katie looked up at her mom. "I want to be able to do this. I want to help."

Cheryl said, "That's a great first step Katie, but why don't we all try to get some sleep. We can discuss more about this tomorrow. Marie and Isabella can share the details about this case and how they've been working with the police."

Marie nodded at Cheryl and said, "Cheryl's right, we can fill you all in on how Isabella has been the main contact with our headless Lawson. Katie, if you're uncomfortable sleeping up here, you can come down with us."

"No, I'll be fine, but I wish I had my camera on, I would have loved to have caught him on tape."

Marie chuckled, placed her hand on Katie's shoulder, and began to guide everyone back to their rooms. "You'll make a great investigator. You can keep the recorder on during the night. It may capture activity going on in the room."

Katie smiled wide, grabbed the camera, and placed it on the nightstand. "That's a great idea."

Jean rolled her eyes toward the other parents and said, "This is going to be a long weekend."

Isabella followed Marie down to the parlor, turned off the lamp, and plopped down on the air mattress. "Marie, why do you think Katie saw Lawson?"

Marie let out a sigh and said, "I'm not sure, Isabella. The only thing I can think of is that spirits are attracted to us because they know we can see and hear them. It's like we're all creating a magnetic force field. They're drawn in."

"I guess, but Megan and Alexi didn't see anything. Don't you think that's weird?"

"I think we need to get some sleep or we're not going to be worth anything tomorrow, okay? See you in the morning, Isabella."

"Okay, good night."

Marie rolled over on her side and knew having these girls on the island may have opened a can of worms with regard to the murders taking place here and on Folly beach. Not only was Isabella keeping something from her, but also Lawson was trying desperately to connect with anyone, which told her there was more he had to say, and that Isabella was the key to that information.

FOURTEEN

MARIE AWOKE to an odd sensation on her hand and realized it was Bailey's tongue in full licking action. She also saw the heel of a foot next to her shoulder and noticed Isabella's head at the foot of the air mattress. Isabella certainly was correct in the fact that she was all over the place when she slept. As she carefully rolled to a sitting position and rubbed Bailey's head, Marie stood up and began her morning routine.

Within a half hour, she heard movement from upstairs and the sound of footsteps on the floors. Marie had coffee brewing and the pre-made egg casserole baking in the oven. The morning sun was warming the back garden making it the perfect day to continue their plans to help these three families accept the gifts they've been given and to learn the tools to control these abilities in their own lives.

The SIPS team slowly arrived one by one and everyone found themselves getting to know each other and share stories of their own paranormal experiences. They first gathered together to discuss the equipment used on ghost investigations, then Cheryl talked with each of the girls and parents separately, and then together. Even Isabella connected with the girls and shared her feelings more openly. Marie still hadn't learned what Isabella was hiding from her, but she knew she would open up when the time was right.

Over the next two days, Marie could see each of the girls coming into their own. Their connections with each other and their parents had lightened. The girls were terrific on the ghost investigation at the fort. They were able to share their abilities and connect with the spirits. They even helped a young girl spirit cross over to her family. It was clear to Marie that creating this weekend for these families was one of the greatest experiences she ever had. She now knew her own journey and planned to continue this in honor of Myra.

With the weekend coming to a close, they decided to gather around the conference table in the SIPS meeting room to discuss the murders taking place on the islands. Cory had scribbled information about the case on the whiteboard, while everyone added their own clues to help find the maniac or maniacs committing these crimes.

"Okay, so you're telling us that each of these victims is connected through the prison. Two were inmates, and the other was a guard." Gale took another sip of her famous margarita and then leaned further back into her chair. "So, whoever brought these guys together is probably who murdered them, but why?"

Tim replied, "I think it has to do with the talents that each of these guys brought to the table. You've got one guy who knew how to make funny money, which would imply spending large amounts for some reason. If Isabella's vision of the cryptogram is the reason, then it would have to lean toward buried treasure."

"Yeah, but what's with the beetle? Do you really think it has to do with Poe's story?" Mimi stared at the plate of cookies and grabbed a piece of fruit instead.

"It makes sense to me." Isabella looked at Marie and continued, "Did anyone try to figure out what the cryptogram means?"

"No actually, but in Poe's story, it talks about Bessop's hostel, which turned out to be some big rock remember? It doesn't exist on the island." Marie stood up, stretched her back, walked over next to Cory, grabbed a marker, and began to write on the board. "Cory interviewed some folks who knew these guys, and it was pretty clear these guys were seedy and dangerous. Kong's statement about Lawson's fear of whoever bailed him out of jail was real. Does anyone know who owns a sword?"

Jim said, "We're not getting anywhere. We still can't tie these guys to anyone. Do you think the murderer is still around?"

"I think he is." Isabella stopped short and then continued, "I just feel like he is."

"Why do you say that, Isabella?" Marie walked over to Isabella and rested her hand on her shoulder. "You must have a reason why you feel that way."

Isabella nervously shrugged her shoulders and shifted in her chair. "I don't know. I just have a feeling."

"If buried treasure is the actual reason behind these murders, has anyone seen or heard of any digging going on here or Folly beach?" Harry straightened his bow tie and pulled out his wrinkled handkerchief to wipe his brow.

"We've already looked into that and came up with zip." Cory set his marker in the tray and leaned against the wall. "Tim and I think there's a connection with how Captain Kidd, or any pirate for that matter, would kill those who knew about the treasure they were hiding. That's the same reason for the myth on Folly Island about the spirit of a pirate haunting anyone who tried to dig up the treasure. With Isabella's connection to Lawson's spirit and the cryptogram, plus the beetle and the hundred-dollar bill shoved down Skerrett's throat, and add to the fact they were beheaded, someone is in search of something and murdered anyone who was involved."

"Maybe we need to quit thinking Poe's story is fiction and follow the coordinates from the cryptogram." Tim looked around the room and then rested his eyes on Isabella. "I think Isabella is the key. Let's pull our resources together and see where these symbols lead us."

Cory said, "That may not be a bad idea. Who knows how to follow the cryptogram?"

Harry raised his hand and said, "I do. I already think I know where to begin. I've been trying to decipher these symbols, and I think the first place to begin is the hill behind the park. These symbols are a bit different from Poe's story."

"That would put us up high enough to look out over the island." Jim popped another pretzel in his mouth and took a sip of ginger ale.

Katie asked, "Are we really going to search for buried treasure?"

Marie chuckled and sat down next to Isabella. "I think we are if everyone is up to it. Isabella, do you think you may be able to get a connection to Lawson? He may be able to help us."

Isabella's leg nervously bounced under the table. "I suppose I can try."

"Do we need shovels?" Gale giggled and finished her margarita.

Marie rolled her eyes and said, "Let's not get carried away. Why don't we all use the facilities and then meet outside? We still have plenty of daylight to start our hunt. It actually may not be a bad idea to bring along some of our cameras and voice recorders. You never know what we may find."

Gale asked, "You're kidding, right? We're seriously going to go treasure hunting?"

"Why not, we've got nothing to lose." Cory winked and wrapped his arm around Marie.

"Have you forgotten how great this team works together to solve crimes? Where's your sense of adventure?" Marie walked with Cory to the door and bent down to clip on Bailey's leash.

Gale replied, "Okay, but I think I'll need to change my shoes."

"Of course you do." Tim lunged back from Gale's flying hand and bumped into the table.

Those who needed to change their shoes did and then met outside. Some carried cameras, others had voice recorders or tablets to take notes. Once the group had assembled, they set out to the hill behind the park, walking in a haphazard path.

Harry stared at the paper containing the cryptogram and stumbled over a shift in the sidewalk. "If I'm correct in what these symbols mean, once we are on the hill, we need to look southeast, which is toward Fort Moultrie."

"Do we know what the coordinates were from Poe's story?" Isabella began to sift through her backpack and pulled out *The Gold Bug*. "I can look it up."

Cory smiled and led the group up the hill, reached the top and faced the fort. "I think any extra information will help us."

"Okay, here's what Legrand says the coordinates represent." Isabella found the page and said, "*A good glass in the bishop's hostel in the devil's seat twenty-one degrees and thirteen minutes northeast and by north main branch seventh limb east side shoot from the left eye of the death's-head a bee line from the tree through the shot fifty-feet out.*"

"Given the fact that the symbols of the cryptogram Isabella wrote down are a bit different, I was able to decipher what each symbol represented in terms of letters and numbers." Harry made it to the top of the hill and stopped short to catch his breath then continued, "We all know bishop's hostel was supposed to be some big rock that had a ledge representing a seat...devil's seat. From my coordinates, we start at this hill and look twenty-one degrees and thirteen minutes southeast, which is at the fort. Now, here's where it gets tricky, in Poe's writings when he stated north main branch seventh limb, he was speaking of a tree. On my findings, it would be southwest of the fort, which puts us in the original grounds of the fort."

Gale rolled her eyes and said, "What exactly does it mean Harry? Where does it put us?"

Harry grabbed his handkerchief, wiped his neck, and shoved the rumpled cloth in his pocket. "I think we need to walk over to the parking area beside the fort and determine the direction from that standpoint."

"You mean to tell me you had us walk all the way up this hill for nothing?" Gale slid her sunglasses down her nose and looked over the rim at Harry.

Isabella said, "Wait a minute, it's a good thing we came up here. Don't we need to look through some binoculars to see exactly which direction from that parking lot? I remember reading that Legrand needed a looking glass."

"She's right." Tim began to walk back down the hill. "I have a pair at the station. I'll be right back."

Megan walked over and stood next to Isabella and peered over her shoulder to read Poe's story. "Do you really think there's buried treasure?"

Katie leaned toward the girls and said, "I think there is."

Tim returned with a pair of binoculars and handed them to Harry. "Take a look and try to pinpoint where exactly in front of that parking lot we need to go."

Harry put the binoculars up to his eyes and began to adjust the focus and then pulled out his compass and held it up toward the fort. "We need to go to the signboard furthest to the left. From there we can locate the next spot."

Gale shook her head and looked at Marie. "Don't you think this large group of people will look suspicious walking around the island with binoculars and compasses and pointing toward the fort?"

"No, we'll just say we're giving our guests a tour." Marie hooked her hand around Cory's arm and began to walk back down the hill.

The group arrived at the spot Harry stated and

assembled around the signboard. Harry pulled out his notes, placed the compass in the palm of his hand, and looked toward the edge of the island. After a few minutes of silence, he placed the paper in his pocket and turned toward the group. "My notes indicate that we need to go to that third palm tree. That should be the final spot."

Katie squealed with the other girls and began to jump up and down. "This is so exciting. Don't you think we're going to need a shovel or something to start digging?"

Megan pulled on Isabella's arm and began to run toward the palm tree. "Come on everyone, what are you waiting for?"

Mimi looked at Jim and tried to hold onto Bailey's leash. "You don't really think it's that simple, do you? Besides, we're on government property."

Jim shrugged his shoulders. "Actually, the palm trees are just outside the border of the park property. To answer your question if I think it's that simple that we're being guided to this spot, I do because when has spirit let us down before?"

Marie said, "He's right Mimi, I think we need to take this information and see if there's anything to it."

"Yeah, but who's to say Harry's directions are right? I mean, he could have screwed up in some of the symbols." Gale looked around at the group and continued, "Or maybe not."

Cheryl walked over to the parents' huddled group and said, "What do you all think? Are you ready to dig for buried treasure?"

Jean shrugged and carefully said, "I'm not really sure I believe in any of this. I remember reading this story, and it was fiction. I don't think it's such a good idea to lead the girls on in this way. Aren't we setting them up for a big fail?"

Cheryl replied, "I believe this is a good thing for them. It's not a matter of actually finding any treasure. It's the camaraderie they are experiencing with each other. It builds their confidence. They're contributing their abilities and that's an important part of their growth and understanding of being psychic. It's important for all of you also."

Katie ran back to the group with wide eyes and said, "Mom, there's a big pile of dirt that looks like it's been dug up. Come on everyone. You have to see this."

Everyone quickly walked over to where Katie and the girls were pointing and there in the spot where Harry's directions led them was a section of ground that looked to be freshly dug and refilled.

Marie looked at Cory and said, "Is this crazy or what? Are we actually onto something?"

Isabella slowly began to sway and in one quick movement stood in a trance-like state. "Lawson is here. He's trying to say something."

Marie placed her index finger to her lips to alert the group to remain quiet. "Isabella, what is he telling you?"

Katie whispered to Jean. "I can see him too."

Marie looked at Katie and smiled. "Can anyone else see or sense Lawson's presence?" After seeing Megan and Alexi nod their heads, she continued, "Isabella, we're all here for you and can help empower your thoughts to understand what Lawson wishes to say. Relax your mind and center on his frequency."

Isabella remained frozen and then opened her eyes and fell against the palm tree. "He's gone, but he said we're in the wrong spot. He said the strangest things."

Marie said, "Don't lose your focus and just repeat exactly what you heard. We'll try to make sense of it."

"Okay, here it goes, he said to stand behind the base of the breech and look past the neck of the columbiad?"

"What the hell does that mean?" Gale placed her sunglasses on the top of her head and peered out toward the fort.

Cory smiled and began to walk toward the parking lot briskly. "I know exactly what it means. Come on, follow me."

Tim jogged in place next to Cory and said, "Are you thinking what I'm thinking?"

"What, what are you both thinking?" Gale tried to keep up with Tim.

Cory walked over to the line of cannons and stood behind the third one in the row and pointed to a knob attached to the cannon. "If I remember correctly, this part here is the knob which is attached at the base of the breech. When you stand here and look out over the cannon, the neck is at the end, and this one particular cannon is a Columbiad. So, my guess is we need to look straight out and use Harry's coordinates again for distance and see where that leads us."

Harry walked over, stood at Cory's spot, pulled out his compass, and set it on the neck of the cannon. "This definitely makes a difference in the coordinates."

Gale rolled her eyes and said, "Don't keep it a secret. Where do we need to go?"

Harry took his eyes off the cannon and said, "Follow me."

Katie grabbed Isabella's arm and pulled her into a run. "Come on. Let's go before it gets too dark."

The group arrived at the spot where Harry stood and searched the ground for any signs of disturbed earth. Mimi let Bailey loose and watched him sniff around where they all stood. After a few minutes, he stopped and began to bark.

Marie stooped down next to Bailey and rubbed his side. "What's the matter, Bailey? Are you picking up on something?"

Jim said, "I wish I had brought my metal detector."

"Metal detector, you mean to tell me you sat on that piece of information and failed to tell us you had something that would help us search for the treasure?" Gale placed her hands on her hips and shook her head.

"Oh, so now you actually think there is treasure?" Megan giggled and huddled behind Katie and Isabella.

Mimi glared at Gale and defensively said, "I don't think you need to get snotty, Gale."

Marie held up her hand. "I think maybe we should call it a day. It's beginning to get dark, so maybe we can pick this up tomorrow? We're all pretty tired."

Katie said, "Do we really want to lose any more time? I think we should go get some flashlights, come back with shovels, and start digging for buried treasure."

Cory shrugged his shoulders. "I tend to agree with Katie. I'd like to see if this takes us anywhere. Jim, can you go and get your metal detector?"

Jim nodded his head. "Absolutely, I can be back here in ten minutes."

"I'll head over to the station and get some flashlights and shovels." Tim began to walk toward the parking lot.

"Okay, I guess we're continuing the search." Marie smiled at Isabella.

"I have to go to the bathroom." Alexi began to shift into a dance and crossed her legs.

Marie pointed toward the fort. "There's a restroom outside of the fort. Isabella, you know where it is, why don't you take her?"

"Okay, I need to go too. Anyone else?"

Katie and Megan nodded their heads and ran with Isabella and Alexi toward the fort. The rest of the group slouched down onto the ground and waited for everyone to return.

Alexi arrived first at the restroom and opened the door. "I'm first."

Isabella said, "There's more than one stall in there."

Megan was last to wash her hands and followed Alexi outside. "That hand dryer blows freezing air."

Isabella walked at the end of the sidewalk and pointed toward a large shrub along the sidewalk. "Is there someone creeping around over there?"

Katie's eyes went into a squint and said, "I can't tell, it's too dark."

A man walked out from the shrub toward the girls and said, "What are all of you doing with that group of people over there?"

Megan squeaked and said, "We're looking for buried treasure."

Isabella's eyes grew wide and shouted. "Shut up

Megan." Isabella gave her attention back to the man and continued, "It's you. You're the murderer. I saw you in my vision. You're the one Lawson said chopped off his head."

The man pulled a pistol from the waist of his jeans, lunged forward, and grabbed Isabella into his arms and ran toward a parked car. The girls screamed waving their hands and ran back to the group.

Marie heard the screams and gave her attention to the girls approaching them in a panic. "What happened? Where's Isabella?"

Katie arrived first and shouted. "Some guy just took Isabella. She said she saw him in her vision and that he's the murderer."

FIFTEEN

"**W**HAT ARE YOU TALKING ABOUT? Slow down and explain to me what just happened." Marie held onto Katie's shoulders and intently stared into her eyes.

"We were coming out of the ladies' room, and Isabella spotted some guy creeping around the bushes, and then he came out and asked us what we were doing with you guys over here." Katie took a deep breath and continued, "Then Isabella started shouting that he was the guy she saw in her vision. The guy that Lawson said chopped off his head."

"Yeah, and then he pulled out a gun and grabbed Isabella and threw her into his car." Megan closed her eyes as the tears slipped down her cheeks and she wiped them off with her sleeves.

Marie saw Cory and Tim running over to join them and then directed her attention back to the girls. "Can any of you describe what this guy looked like and what kind of a car he was driving?"

Alexi began to shake and plopped down onto the ground, landing in a cross-legged position. "He was tall and thin, and I think his hair was dark."

"Yeah, and he wore glasses." Megan sat down

next to Alexi and wrapped her arm around Alexi's shoulders.

Marie explained the situation to Cory and Tim and again turned her attention back to the girls and asked, "What did the glasses look like? Do you remember the make or color of the car?"

Katie said, "His glasses were dark-framed, and they were round. His car looked like it was maybe dark blue or black. I couldn't make out what kind of car it was, but it had four doors."

"So, it wasn't an SUV, it was more of a sedan?" Gale stooped down next to Alexi and lightly rubbed her back.

"Yeah, it looked more like a sedan." Alexi looked up at Marie. "Is she going to be okay? Should we have gone after him?"

Cory replied, "Absolutely not, you girls did exactly what you should have done. I'm going to call this in and head over to the station. Marie, I think maybe it'd be best if you all head back to Myra's place. You'll also need to contact Caroline. She's going to need to know what just happened to her daughter."

Gale looked at Marie and said, "Doesn't that sound like Professor Cooper?"

Marie quickly yanked Cory's sleeve and pulled him over next to Gale. "That's exactly what I was going to say. He's tall and thin and wears round vintage glasses. He also drives a blue Mercedes sedan."

Cory said, "He does fit that profile, but I think we need to have more to go on than a possible hunch."

"Can we find a picture of him somewhere that we could show the girls? Now I know what it was that Isabella was hiding from Adam and me. This is what she saw, and I should have picked up on it." Marie held back tears and blankly looked at Cory and Gale.

Cory pulled Marie into his chest and held her tight. "Marie, you know this isn't your fault."

"She's my responsibility. I promised her mother I'd look after her. I should have pried it out of her." Marie looked up at Cory and said, "I need to go with you. I need to be there for Isabella if this creep has her."

Jim ran over from the palm tree and said, "I think you need to come over here. My metal detector found something."

Marie jogged back with Cory and Gale and peered down into the hole Jim had dug and winced at the sight she saw. "Oh wow, is that a head?"

Cory replied, "Something tells me we just found the rest of Freddie Stuart."

Gale pointed and curled up her lips. "Are those two gold coins shoved in the eye sockets?"

Jim said, "Yeah, that's exactly what they are. Do you think the murderer found the buried treasure here and then chopped off Stuart's head? Just like Captain Kidd?"

"It's hard to say, but I'm radioing this in, everyone needs to stand back and don't touch anything. Mimi, can you please take everyone back to Myra's house? I need to clear this crime scene." Cory carefully looked at Marie and said, "I want you to go back to the house also."

"I can't go back to the house now. Not with Isabella being taken. We don't know what Cooper's going to do with her, but I think we know he's capable of anything." Marie pulled her arm away from Cory and jammed her hands on her hips. "We need to move fast. We have to go and search his house. We're losing time."

"First of all, we have no idea that it is Cooper. We can't just go rushing into his house without probable cause and a warrant. You know that." Cory moved close to Marie and stroked her cheek with the back of his hand. "But I also know your hunches and that you're not going to go back to Myra's house. I at least had to say it."

Marie slowly smiled and kissed Cory's cheek. "Thank you. I'm searching now on my phone for any news articles that may have a picture of Cooper to show the girls. If they identify him as the guy who took Isabella, is that enough probable cause?"

"Yes, and in the meantime, I need to call this in and get this marked as a crime scene. If they do identify him, I'll get the judge to issue a warrant to search Cooper's residence." Cory kissed Marie's nose and grabbed his cell phone to make the call.

Marie saw Mimi gather the girls and their parents back to Myra's place and then walked over to Gale and Tim. "Help me search for a news article to find a picture of Cooper. There has to be one when he donated money for Thompson Park. If we find one, send it to Mimi so she can show the girls. If this is who they saw, Cory's going to get a warrant to search his house."

Gale asked, "You don't really think he's there, do you? He must know that'd be the first place they'd look for him."

"I know, but there may be clues there to help tie him to these murders. I'm going to go with Cory. I need to be there for Isabella. Can you two stay with everyone back at Myra's?"

Gale placed her hand on Marie's shoulder. "Of course we will. Look, Marie this isn't your fault, you do know that, don't you?"

"I'm trying to tell myself that. It just frustrates me that I haven't been able to pick up on anything with this case. Myra isn't even around to help me." Marie quickly wiped the tears from her face and shook her head. "Okay, I need to focus, enough of the pity party. Let me know if you find any pictures of Cooper. I'm going to go with Cory."

Tim said, "We're on it."

ISABELLA SCREAMED, kicked, and tried to keep him from putting her in the boat. "Let go of me. Where are you taking me?"

He shoved the pistol against her temple and said, "You need to shut up and stop kicking me. Now do as you're told and get in the boat. We're going for a little cruise, and if you don't stop fighting me, I'll shoot you right here."

Isabella began to sob and stepped into the fishing boat then stood against the port side. "They're going to find me. Marie's a better psychic than I am, and she'll find me, and they'll put on death row."

He grabbed a roll of duct tape, tore off a piece and shoved it over Isabella's mouth. "You don't know what you're talking about. Marie's no more psychic than that crazy old lady friend of hers, now shut up and sit down. I need to think, and I can't concentrate with you babbling on about stupid shit."

· · ·

GALE'S EYES got large and yelled at Marie and Tim. "I found a picture of Cooper. Take a look."

Marie glanced at the image on Gale's phone and smiled. "Perfect. Send it to Mimi and have her check with the girls to see if this is the guy they saw take Isabella."

Gale sent the image to Mimi as a text. "Okay, she has it. I told her to make it quick we're losing time."

Marie heard the alert and looked at Gale. "Well?"

"It's a match. He's the guy. Go tell Cory."

Marie hugged Gale tight and ran over to Cory. "The girls identified Cooper as the guy who took Isabella."

"Great, I have Tom waiting on stand-by at Judge Dougherty's office to get the warrant. As soon as he has it, we'll meet him over at Cooper's place."

"How long will that take?"

"Not long, don't worry. We're going to find her. I promise."

Gale walked with Tim over to Marie and said, "We're going to head back to Myra's now. If you need anything at all you call us, okay?"

"I will and thank you."

Tim smiled and rubbed Marie's arm. "Don't worry. Cory's going to find her."

Cory walked over to Marie and grabbed her elbow. "Come on. Tom has the warrant. We're headed over to Cooper's place now."

Marie waved at Gale and Tim and then jumped in next to Cory in his police car. She began to rub her temples and took a deep breath. "I've been trying to clear my mind to see if I can get any kind of a read from Lawson or Myra. I'm just batting zero with all of this."

"You know that I believe in your abilities more than anyone. But I've always been a man of evidence and science. We may just come up with something at Cooper's house that will lead us in the right direction." Cory grabbed Marie's hand off the seat and kissed her fingertips. "I believe in you. Now you need to trust me in what I do, okay?"

Marie smiled and then turned her attention to the driveway of Cooper's house. "I know, and I do. Now let's see what this creep has hidden inside."

Cory put the car in park and grabbed Marie's arm. "We need to wait for Tom with the warrant and some backup before we can go anywhere. Plus, you're going to stay here until it's clear for you to come in because I have a feeling we're going to need your *abilities* if we find anything inside that you can use your psychometry. I'm going to have a look around until Tom gets here."

"Gee, what happened to evidence and science?" Marie chuckled and poked Cory's ribs.

Cory laughed and saw a car approach them with flashing blue and red lights. "There's Tom, now remember, wait here until I tell you it's clear to come inside."

Marie gave a tilted salute and said, "Aye aye captain."

Cory shook his head, got out of the car, released his pistol from the holster, and nodded to Tom to follow. After a few minutes, he came back out of the house and waved at Marie to come inside.

Marie tentatively walked through the opened front door and began to look around the immaculate kitchen. "It doesn't even look as though anyone lives here. It's so clean."

Cory crooked his finger and said, "You need to see what we found in a room that was padlocked."

Marie followed Cory and Tom into a back room and gasped. "Oh my, what the hell is all of this?"

"It looks to be a collection of things our professor has either found on archeological digs or stole." Cory moved out of the way of the forensic team that arrived and handed a pair of latex gloves to Marie. "Take a look at the swords over on the wall and these maps. Let's hope they've got traces of blood that match our victims. There's also a bug collection over there. Now we know where the beetle came from."

Marie slipped on the gloves and looked around the room. "What are these bones from?"

"Hard to say, but I suspect those aren't from any ruins." Cory picked up a gold coin and turned it around on his latex fingers and held it under the light. "This thing is dated eighteen forty-one."

Marie's eyebrows went up as she glanced at the coin. "Do you really think he found buried treasure somewhere?"

"I don't know, but why don't you hold it and see if you're able to come up with anything."

Marie reached for the coin when her cell phone rang causing her to jump and drop the coin. "Sorry, it's Gale calling." Marie answered the phone and said, "Hey, what's up? Yeah, we've found a bunch of stuff. They did what? Are you kidding me? Morris Island? Are you sure? Yeah, okay I'll tell Cory, bye, and Gale...thanks."

"What'd she say?"

"You're never going to guess what happened. Katie, Megan, and Alexi did a mini-séance and contacted Lawson. He just told them Cooper has Isabella at the Morris Island lighthouse."

"Morris Island? There's no way of getting there other than by boat. Are you really sure they understood the message?" Cory stopped short and said, "Okay, by the look you just gave me that was a very stupid question. Let me get Tom and a few patrolmen and let's head on over to the island."

ISABELLA CAUTIOUSLY STEPPED out of the rocking boat and landed her foot on the dock in front of the Morris Island Lighthouse. She struggled against his hand pulling her over the tall metal sheet piles as she landed hard on her feet on the inside facing the lighthouse. She grimaced at the pain that shot up through her ankles and then caught the light from the moon shining onto the no trespassing sign.

He yanked the duct tape from her mouth and laughed at her scream from the pain. "You can scream all you want. Nobody's going to hear you. Now follow that path over to the lighthouse. I have some things I need to get before I decide what to do with you."

MARIE NERVOUSLY BIT her lip as she listened to the sirens of the police car hum in her ears. She questioned her abilities and wondered why she wasn't able to connect with anyone on the other side of the veil to help them solve this case. She felt a sense of failure in keeping Isabella safe and remembered her fear when she lost Myra to a demon. She quickly dismissed that fear and repeated in her head that she would not allow any harm to come to Isabella. It wasn't going to happen today.

Cory quickly glanced over at Marie. "I know what's going on in that beautiful head of yours. You can stop thinking any of this is your fault. You weren't the one Lawson chose to communicate with. You've told me many times before that nobody has control over that. We're going to find her and bring her back safe. Cooper has no idea we're coming."

Marie faintly smiled and lovingly looked at the man she committed her life to only a few weeks before. "I know, and I believe in my heart that we're going to find her alive and well. I won't allow it to happen any other way."

Cory nodded his head and grabbed the radio and spoke to the units following behind. "I want everyone to kill their lights and sirens as we approach the end of the beach. I want the boat crew unit to move on ahead and suit up."

Marie fell forward against her seatbelt from the force of the car jerking to a stop. She released the belt and jumped out of the car. She saw men and women running to their positions and glanced over at Cory. "You *are* going to allow me to go with you on that boat, aren't you?"

Cory winced and pursed his lips together and remained silent for a few seconds, and then said, "Marie, you know that's against all protocol. I can't allow you to get on that boat. You're going to have to trust me and these units to bring Isabella back safe. You know I'd do anything for you, but I can't allow you to get on that boat."

Marie knew she wasn't going to persuade him to change his mind and nodded her head in agreement.

"I know, and I do trust you, all of you, but I want you to stay in radio contact with me."

"I will when I'm able to communicate. We're going to be on radio silence until we've got Cooper in custody. Let's hope the girls got it right and he's there with Isabella." Cory walked over to Marie after securing his life vest and cupped her face in his hands. "I love you more than you can imagine, and I know what's running through your mind. No fear, right?"

"Right...no fear." Marie returned his kiss and watched him disappear into the night at the ocean's edge.

She tightly held onto the radio and quietly asked her spirit guides to protect the men and women risking their lives to save Isabella. As she watched the moonlight dance on the ocean waves, she impatiently waited to hear any sound from Cory that their mission was over, and they were heading back to land.

It felt like hours when suddenly static vibrated on the radio and Marie heard a scared female voice say, "Marie, it's me, Isabella. I'm okay. They're bringing me back."

Marie's face flooded with tears as she pushed in the button and said, "Isabella, I'm here. I'm so glad you're okay. Are you hurt?"

"No, I'm fine, they caught him by surprise. Marie, he's dead, he shot himself in the head."

Marie could hear Isabella's sobs, and she stooped down on the ground and leaned against the car. "You don't worry about that now. You just listen to Chief Miller and everything will be fine."

There was silence and then a male voice said, "Marie, it's me, Cory, Isabella's fine. We're bringing her back first and then going back for Cooper's body, along with enough gold, diamonds, and silver to balance the countries debt."

Marie began to laugh uncontrollably and looked up at the sky and silently mouthed the words thank you.

MARIE ROLLED her suitcase into the kitchen and sadly looked at Bailey. "Don't make me feel any worse than I do boy. If I could take you to Paris, I would. You know that."

Gale rolled her eyes and said, "Oh man, you two are so pitiful. Between Tim, Mimi, and I, he'll be fine."

Cory joined them in the kitchen and placed the smaller bags on the counter. "I'm just blown away we were able to organize two weeks in France with our schedules."

"Yeah, well it's only because you were able to solve this case." Tim leaned against the counter next to Gale. "Who would have thought there was buried treasure on the island?"

Gale raised one eyebrow and said, "It wasn't really buried treasure. It was stolen. I can't believe Cooper wasn't arrested sooner. How he was able to get away after all these years stealing museum artifacts and then burying it all around on these islands is beyond me. Not to mention how many people he murdered along the way. Are they done finding bodies on Folly Island?"

"The last count I heard was twelve. They've only just begun matching them to the missing person's database. I would imagine they were people he befriended along the way that could help him one way or another to steal the artifacts. Because of his profession as an archeologist, he was able to get away with doing digs and getting permission to places most people weren't. It looks like the vision Marie had before the wedding referred to *these* bodies." Cory stuffed the plane tickets in his shirt pocket.

Tim asked, "But why did he go to such great lengths with the cryptogram and maps and the whole pirate theme?"

"It's hard to say, and we may never know. He murdered everyone involved and then by shooting himself, took that piece of information with him." Cory looked at his watch. "We'd better get going. We need to be at the airport a couple of hours before takeoff."

Gale said, "Yeah, well I'll say it again, Cooper was a nut. I'm just glad Isabella's okay, and Caroline wasn't angry with any of us."

Marie said, "I had a long talk with both of them. Cheryl was a big help too. I think Isabella was more excited she was able to help. She'll be fine. She felt bad for not telling us that Lawson showed her Cooper's face in a vision, but she was too scared. Plus, she really didn't know who he was. It was all pretty confusing for her. I also got emails from Alexi, Megan, and Katie. They all made it home safe and sound."

Marie and Cory said their goodbyes and loaded their luggage into the car. Marie waved and then turned her attention to Cory and smiled. They were finally going on their honeymoon. She leaned her head back and thought back to how this all began and realized how much she had learned. Not to mention how much she and the SIPS team accomplished, with more of the kudos going to Isabella.

Not only were they able to help solve the case, but also, they were able to help Isabella learn to handle her abilities and build her confidence, *and* she was a new member of SIPS. They also created a retreat for psychic kids and their families. Marie developed a great friendship with Katie, Megan, Alexi, and their parents. She knew the girls had a sense of pride to have been able to help find Isabella. They all shared their desire to go on helping others with their abilities.

Yes, this was to be her destiny, her role in life, but for now, all she wanted to think about was sharing that moment when she and her husband saw the Eiffel Tower for the first time.

Dear reader,

We hope you enjoyed reading *Secret of Coffin Island*. Please take a moment to leave a review, even if it's a short one. Your opinion is important to us.

Discover more books by Robin Murphy at https://www.nextchapter.pub/authors/robin-murphy

Want to know when one of our books is free or discounted? Join the newsletter at http://eepurl.com/bqqB3H

Best regards,

Robin Murphy and the Next Chapter Team

ABOUT THE AUTHOR

Robin Murphy has worked in the administrative, graphic design, desktop publishing, writing, and self-publishing realm for more than thirty-five years. Her wide range of skills and abilities place her at the top of her field.

The first book in her paranormal mystery series is SULLIVAN'S SECRET, the second book is Secret of the Big Easy, the third is Federal City's Secret, and the fifth is SAVANNAH'S SECRET. She is also a freelance and travel writer.

Robin has been a speaker on author platforms, self-publishing, and marketing,. She has also written A Complete "How To" Guide for Rookie Writers, which is a very practical, hands-on and user-friendly book to enable a rookie writer to learn how to get their newly created work produced and available to readers, as well as, a comedic romance titled, *Point and Shoot for Your Life*, which was a ReadFree.Ly 2016 Best Indie Book Finalist.

You can find Robin's books on **Amazon**.

ALSO BY ROBIN MURPHY

Secret Of Coffin Island
ISBN: 978-4-86747-856-1
Mass Market

Published by
Next Chapter
1-60-20 Minami-Otsuka
170-0005 Toshima-Ku, Tokyo
+818035793528

28th May 2021

Lightning Source UK Ltd.
Milton Keynes UK
UKHW041023170621
385669UK00001B/30

9 784867 478561